THE 12 FRIGHTS OF CHRISTMAS

For Mom
an

INTRODUCTION

I love Christmas. I love everything about it – the preparation, the decorations, the feeling of joy and goodwill... and the food.

I have another love – horror. I love all things slimy, slithery and bump in the nighty. My favourite present to find under the tree on Christmas morning is a horror novel.

It seems rather strange to be writing an introduction to a book of Christmas-themed horror stories with the air conditioning on full and the sun blazing away outside. But such is the nature of publishing cycles.

The tradition of Christmas-themed horror goes back centuries. In Victorian times, the telling of ghost stories on Christmas Eve was a much-loved tradition. Charles Dickens' A Christmas Carol is, at its very core, a classic ghost story. I watch it every year on Christmas Eve – but only the 1953 classic with Alistair Sim as the infamous miser. Any other version pales in comparison.

You will find a few ghosts in this book, but there are also sinister Santas, terrifying trees and nefarious nutcrackers.

There have been many more modern offerings around the theme of horrible things happening at the most wonderful time of the year: Ghost Story by Peter Straub, The Shining by Stephen King, NOAS42 by Joe Hill and Let the Right One In by John Ajvide Lindquivst, to name but a few. And we can't forget all those scary Christmas movies: Gremlins, Black Christmas, Krampus, Anna and the Apocalypse, The Lodge, Jack Frost and Silent Night, Deadly Night. Perfect to snuggle up with a cup of hot chocolate and a pile of presents to wrap. Just be careful with those scissors… they look pretty sharp.

Winter in my part of the world brings long dark nights and bitter cold. We chase it away with the warmth of a fireplace and the glow of Christmas lights.

But what if there is something lurking behind that glow? Maybe in those shadows where the light doesn't quite reach? Did you hear something creaking between the first and second verses of Good King Wenceslas? It might have been the wind.

It seems like it's gotten a bit colder in here. Like there's a draft coming in through an open door. I'd better go check. I'll be right back.

Merry Christmas.

Lenore Butcher

June 2023

COUNTDOWN TO CHRISTMAS

The countdown to Christmas truly can begin at any time. It's more than just the decorations. It's also a state of mind. For me, the countdown to next year's Christmas actually begins during Boxing Week of the previous Christmas. That's because I start my shopping for next Christmas at the Boxing Week sales. I know. I kind of hate me a little bit too right now.

In our house, while the countdown to Christmas begins much earlier, our official preparations don't officially begin until November 12. My husband, a veteran of our Armed Forces, does not believe in allowing Christmas cheer to overshadow the solemnity of Remembrance Day.

A lot of kids start counting down to Christmas on November 1st. That could just be the sugar high from Hallowe'en talking. Some people mark the start of advent season with a calendar, or special church sessions. Still others know that Christmas is truly on the way when pumpkin spice season gives way to cranberry season at the coffee shops.

No matter how you mark it, the people in the next four stories are all counting down to Christmas in very different ways and for very different reasons…

NUTS

My husband collects Nutcrackers. I think they're spooky!

"Where did you find such a hideous thing?"

Charlie finished folding the paper away from her new treasure before she answered Bryan. "I was walking past that funky little store on Light Street. The one that smells like patchouli and grease. There he was in the window. It was like he was waiting for me to come for him." She put the nutcracker statue on the mantel beside the many others she'd amassed over the years. She shifted some of his fellows aside to make room for him in the platoon.

The nutcracker's flat black eyes and painted on grin stared vacantly in Bryan's direction. He felt uneasy the longer he gazed at it, but he couldn't bring himself to look away. The jacket was an indeterminate colour between a mossy green and an electric blue. The trousers were a mottled red colour with uneven flecks of darker red dotting the surface.

Charlie carefully put the tissue back into the box and set it aside. "Can you put this box in the storage closet? I have to go get ready for my office party tonight."

"I'd forgotten that was tonight." Bryan dragged his gaze away from the nutcracker, thankful to have something else to focus on.

"Yes. Want to come along?" Charlie made the offer with the air of one who already knows the answer.

"Thanks, but no." The last thing he wanted to do was stand around the meeting room at the Quality Inn, sipping on his two free complimentary watered-down cocktails and listening to the women from the accounting firm where Charlie worked gossiping about anyone who wasn't at the party and asking Charlie sympathetically, "No ring yet, Charlene? It's been what… six years now?"

Eight. But he'd propose when he was damn good and ready and not because Marnie from reception couldn't stop asking every year.

"All right." Charlie kissed his cheek. "I'm just going to go get ready."

Bryan settled back in his chair. He picked up his cell phone. He would play a few hands of poker just to relax while Charlie got ready. Once she left for her party, he was going to wrap her Christmas presents.

There was a hollow popping noise from the mantel. Bryan first looked down at the empty hearth. There were logs stacked neatly inside. He had laid a fire on. He knew that Charlie would return from her office party, drunk and giggling from several rounds of Cosmopolitans. Experience with drunk Charlie had led Bryan to discover that laying a fire was a sure way to get him laid.

But the fire was hours from now. There wasn't anything in the fireplace to make that popping sound. His gaze drifted upwards to the display of nutcrackers that marched across the faux white marble top of the mantle. There were nine of them, ranked in size with the largest in the center and then fanning out to the smallest at each end. Charlie's new one was on the left, third from the center.

His mouth was gaping open. As horrible as his painted-on sneer had been, the void revealed by the dropping of the hinged jaw was infinitely worse. The yaw seemed to grow. It dominated Bryan's vision until all he could see was darkness and something small and white and unholy squirming in the depths.

"Hey."

Bryan flinched and swallowed his startled shriek at Charlie's voice. She leaned over him, concerned.

"Are you okay? You look rattled."

"I'm fine." It was lunacy to be afraid of a toy. "Just watching something creepy on TikTok." He waved his phone. He tried to smile convincingly at her. "You look great. Is that a new dress?"

She nodded. "I picked it up last weekend. I'm heading out soon, but I've got some snacks for you. I'll put them out before I go."

"You always take such good care of me." He smiled at Charlie. She bustled to the kitchen.

Snik.

The sound was very faint above the rush of blood in his ears, but loud enough to get his attention.

The nutcracker's mouth was closed again, sealing off the abyss within.

Maybe he'd just imagined it. He was letting his overworked brain see things that weren't there. Or maybe the nutcracker had a faulty joint.

"Here we go." Charlie handed him a pint glass full of amber fluid. She set a bowl of party mix on the table in front of him. "There's also nuts in the basket and candy in the candy dish." She nodded at the two receptacles on the coffee table. "I shouldn't be long. I've got to at least put in an appearance."

He would normally tell her to take her time and have fun, but tonight he didn't want her to go. He didn't want to be alone in the apartment with the empty stares and smiles surrounding him.

"Wait."

She turned back. "Changed your mind? Want to tag along?"

He opened his mouth, then he shook his head. He wasn't going to derail his evening plans by giving in to a momentary fancy. "Nothing. Have a good time."

Once Charlie had left, Bryan headed into the dining room. He'd hidden Charlie's Christmas presents in the credenza. He laid them out on the shining surface of their table. A cashmere scarf. The newest hardcover from Kelley Armstrong. And a small box from her favourite upscale jewelry store. He opened the lid, taking a moment to admire the pair of perfect emerald earrings nestled in the velvety folds. He knew it was kind of a jerk move to give her earrings when he knew she'd been expecting an engagement ring for years. Bryan was kind of a jerk. He prided himself on it.

He started wrapping the scarf. Movement in his peripheral vision drew his attention.

A walnut sat in the middle of the floor under the archway that connected the living room to the dining room.

"Must've fallen out of the nut dish," Bryan muttered. He abandoned his wrapping project to fetch the nut. He cast a wary glance at the array of nutcrackers.

All mouths were shut. All eyes were glassy and vacant. Bryan stooped to put the walnut in the basket.

Pop.

The mouth was open again. Bryan's fingers loosened on the walnut. It bounced against the coffee table with a clatter, then careened off into the murky depths under the couch.

He stared into that dreadful chasm for as long as he dared. He had to look away because he could feel it calling him, drawing him in.

Snik.

The mouth was closed when he reluctantly looked again.

He couldn't stand here forever staring at the nutcracker.

It would look so foolish if Charlie came home and he was still transfixed in front of this toy. He returned to the dining room.

He was just reaching for the tape to secure the paper around the scarf box when he happened to glance up.

Pop.

The nut was back. Or maybe it was a different nut. Either way, a walnut sat right on the narrow strip of trim that divided the dining room from whatever madness was unfolding in the living room.

He'd never noticed how much the surface of a walnut felt like a brain. His fingertips recoiled from the texture of bumps and grooves. He kept his eyes averted from the mantle as he hurried to the coffee table to deposit the nut in the basket. He didn't want to know what was going on in the troops so neatly arrayed along that narrow ledge.

The walnut's burnished surface stood out against the background of shelled nuts in the basket – an assortment of peanuts, cashews, almonds, and Brazil nuts. Not a walnut in the lot shelled or otherwise.

Snik.

Bryan looked at the nutcracker again. Had it shifted position on the mantle? Was it just a smidge closer to the edge? The corners of the nutcracker's mouth seemed to have lifted a bit, making the mindless smile wider and more malevolent. He didn't want to touch the horrible thing, but he couldn't stand having it in his house, let alone the living room for a moment longer. It had to go.

It was still five days until Christmas. He had lots of time to buy Charlie a new scarf. He wrapped the scarf around the nutcracker, thrust it into the box and hurled it into the storage closet by their bedroom. He felt better once he'd slammed the door. Tomorrow he'd convince Charlie to take it back to the store.

He paused in the bathroom to wash his hands and give himself a stern talking to in the mirror. He'd dealt with the nutcracker. If Charlie was unhappy with it, he could deal with her too.

Once he'd regained his composure, he headed towards the dining room. A ribald chorus of *pops* and *sniks* heralded his progress through the living room. He kept his eyes forward, not looking to the mantle. If he saw a row of open, gaping mouths, he was going to lose it. That was a certainty.

The hell with it. He could meet Charlie at her company party. Maybe he could even book them a room for the night at the hotel. He could even splurge for a suite if that's what it took. He could use his powers of persuasion to convince her to take the nutcracker back. He didn't even care if she could get a refund on the damned thing – it just had to go.

The storage closet door was ajar. One panicked look inside assured him the box with the nutcracker in it was still there. He could see it upended in the furthest darkest corner, resting on top of his golf clubs and Charlie's old ice skates. He shut the door firmly and put a heavy book against the base, preventing any egress from a possessed trinket.

In the bedroom he quickly changed from his sweatpants and t-shirt into a pair of dress slacks and Charlie's favourite sweater. She said it made his eyes "pop". No. He wasn't going to thing about the word "pop". He stripped off the sweater and chose a dress shirt, one with a nice subtle blue stripe. He had to look nice. He grabbed his cufflinks from his jewelry box. He didn't usually wear them, but Charlie had given him this pair for Christmas last year and he'd never worn them. It was time. One cufflink escaped his shaking fingers and skittered under the bed. Cursing, he dropped to his knees, reaching for it.

Pop.

His gaze was drawn down the length of his body, to the

object now nestled between his splayed-out knees. There was hungry malice in those dark eyes and greed in that gaping maw. The nutcracker was after a different sort of sweet meat.

Snik.

PUMPKIN SPICE FEVER

Some ladies will do anything to get their Pumpkin Spice fix...

Eva announced her arrival as she always did – a single insouciant blast of her horn as she used her key fob to lock the doors of her ridiculously overpriced and overly accessorized silver Escalade.

The rising wind eddied her through the doors of the little café. At just after two on a weekday afternoon, the quaint little eatery was almost empty, save for the staff and the two women waiting for Eva.

"Here she comes," Suzanne muttered under her breath. Suzanne had her back to the door, so Eva did not see her lips mouthing along to Eva's typical greetings, much to Fern's entertainment.

"Sorry I'm late. Traffic was murder. Mwah. Mwah." She over-exaggerated the noise as she "air kissed" in the general vicinity of each of her friends' cheeks. She dropped easily into the chair between Fern and Suzanne, turning her head to address the server hovering attentively nearby.

"Harvest salad and pumpkin spice latte." She turned back to her friends. "Now. You won't believe what Greg…"

The server cleared her throat uncomfortably. "Umm…"

"What?" There was an edge to Eva's voice. She did not like being interrupted.

"We. Umm…" The poor girl was melting under Eva's baleful glare. "We don't have those…" The words tumbled out in a rush.

"You don't have what?" Eva demanded.

The girl fidgeted, her hands twining in front of her, fingers curling around each other nervously. "The drink or the salad. We don't carry those."

Eva barked a sharp laugh. "What do you mean? Of course you do. I've ordered the same thing every Thursday since Labour Day. "

The girl looked down at the toes of her shoes, obviously wishing she were anywhere else but standing in front of the angry woman who'd just found out she was going to be denied her pumpkin spice latte. "Yes Ma'am."

"I had it just last Thursday."

"Yes. Only last Thursday was November thirtieth."

"And?" Eva tapped her fingernail impatiently on the table.

"And we switched on Friday. To our festive menu. Because it's December now and we--"

"Your what now?" Eva stopped tapping to stare at the hapless server.

"Our festive menu. You could have a gingerbread latte. And our warm cranberry salad. It's really good." The server tried to give Eva a cheerful smile, drum up some enthusiasm for the menu selections she was offering.

The angry wrinkle that appeared in her forehead when Eva was thwarted was in full display. "But it's not what I want."

The server shrugged helplessly. "I'm sorry?"

Eva sighed in resignation. "Fine. Fine." She flapped one dismissive hand at the girl. "I'll take the gingerbread thing and the cranberry whatever."

Relieved to be released, the server scurried back to the kitchen to put their orders in.

"So. Now let me tell you about the shit Greg pulled today..." For the next fifteen minutes Eva took centre stage as she usually did at their lunches, holding forth on the never-ending saga of her trials and tribulations with her work "frenemy" Greg.

By the time she'd finished her breathless account of her recent triumph over Greg's pettiness in the battlefield of the boardroom, their drinks and meals had arrived.

Eva took a tentative sip of her drink and then picked indifferently at the edges of her salad.

"How is it?" Fern asked.

"All right..." Eva sighed, using her fork to push several grains of quinoa into a nest of cilantro. "It's definitely not my usual." She took another dispirited sip of her drink. "I'd kill for a pumpkin spice latte."

"Mine's good." Fern offered up her opinion even though Eva hadn't asked. She had the same salad. "Suzanne, how's the turkey sandwich?"

"So good. And I love the home-made potato chips." Suzanne crunched a few for emphasis.

"Ladies." A tall man with a neatly trimmed goatee and dark eyes stopped by their table. "I'm Franklin, the manager. How is everything?"

Suzanne and Fern mumbled their appreciation around mouths full of food.

Eva sighed theatrically. "I'd kill for a pumpkin spice latte."

Franklin's smile widened. His dark red lips parted to reveal almost unnaturally white teeth. "Would you now?" He chuckled and it made Fern and Suzanne squirm uneasily. "I think I can arrange that..."

Franklin left their table and passed through the swinging door into the kitchen. Voices were raised and it sounded like an argument. Silence reigned after Franklin's deep voice rumbled something that sounded like it was part threat, part command.

Fern's salad suddenly felt like a lead weight in her stomach. Suzanne pushed her plate away. Fern guessed that Suzanne was feeling the same uneasiness. Maybe the machine that had brewed their lattes hadn't been cleaned properly. She couldn't wait to pay their bill and get out of her, out into the fresh air.

Eva didn't look sick. In fact, she'd perked up a bit. She was watching the kitchen door expectantly.

Franklin soon returned, carrying a tray. It held a steaming white ceramic mug and a folded towel. He set the tray down on a nearby table and brought the mug to Eva.

"Here we are." He set the mug in front of her with a great deal of ceremony. He produced a shaker and dusted the top of the drink with fresh nutmeg.

She bent over and closed her eyes. She inhaled deeply. "So wonderful." She took her first sip. Her face blossomed into a beaming smile.

"This is absolutely the best pumpkin spice latte I've ever had."

Franklin smiled. "I added a special ingredient. Just for you."

"You should definitely market this. It's absolutely perfect."

"It's under consideration." He waited while she took another swallow. "More nutmeg?" He offered the shaker to her.

She shook her head. "No, this is great. I'm not really a big nutmeg fan, so this is just enough." She took another sip and then another, humming her pleasure at the taste.

"More nutmeg?" He held the shaker out again.

This time she took it from him. Her hand trembled slightly as she shook a few specks out into the half-empty mug.

"A little more," he suggested. Her fingers moved jerkily, adding another powdering of the spice.

"I thought you didn't like nutmeg?" Suzanne stared at Eva.

"It's better with a bit more, isn't it, Eva?" Franklin murmured. His hand came to rest on Eva's shoulder. Suzanne and Fern waited for her to shrug it off, to protest, to use this uninvited familiarity to finagle a free beverage or meal comp. It was Eva's usual response to a "service person" overstepping their "place".

Eva nodded, mumbling, "Good" and taking another drink. She drained the remainder of the beverage. Her eyes were a bit glazed as she set the empty mug down. "I know I should've savoured it. But it was so good…"

"I'll make you another," he promised. "But why don't you take off your blouse first?"

"My—" Eva's voice was uncertain. "Why?"

"Eva don't…" Fern muttered. She reached to put her hand on Eva's wrist. "Don't do it. Let's just go…"

"Oh, I'm afraid there's still the little matter of the bill…" Franklin kept his hand on Eva's shoulder. "Someone needs to pay."

Eva fumbled for the clasp on her clutch. His other hand moved to rest on hers. "I don't want your money, Eva."

"Then what?"

"Your blouse. Please. It's very hot in here. Don't you feel how hot it is? Eva?"

"Hot…" Her fingers began to work the buttons on her blouse.

Fern and Suzanne exchanged desperate looks. They didn't know what was going on here, what sort of crazy hold this bizarre man had on Eva but things were getting stranger by the second.

"Eva…" Suzanne tried to get her friends attention. Eva kept

undoing her blouse, her eyes fixed on the tablecloth.

Eva finished undoing her blouse and handed it to Franklin. He smoothed his fingers over the tracings of silver embroidery that decorated the front.

"Such a pretty blouse," he mused, "It would be a terrible shame to get it messy." Franklin placed the blouse carefully on the table next to theirs. "You're almost ready for what comes next, aren't you Eva?"

"Ready for another pumpkin latte? Yes." She nodded unsteadily. "I would very much like another pumpkin latte…" Eva's voice drifted into wispy tatters. It was very unlike her usual brassy, commanding vibrato.

"Not quite yet." Franklin reached over to fetch the towel from the other table. Suzanne thought he might be intending to clean away the spots where Eva had slopped her latte in her haste to drink it all down.

The famous Eva pout was back, even if her stare was vacant and glassy. "You promised…"

"As soon as you hold up your end of the bargain…" His hand reached into the depths of the towel.

"My what?" Eva was confused. She swayed a bit. Her eyes seemed to be drifting away, out of focus. Fern wondered uneasily what the "special ingredient" had been that Franklin had alluded to when he brought Eva her coveted drink.

Franklin showed Eva what he held in his hand. The knife had a heavy wooden handle with a long silver blade curved into a wicked smile. Franklin held it higher, letting the sharp crescent glitter in the diffuse amber glow of the overhead lights. He let it fall from his hand. It landed in front of Eva with a heavy thud. She looked from the knife and back up to Franklin looming over her. She had a dazed look on her face, like she'd lost all touch with reality, with who she was and where she was.

"You did say you'd kill for a pumpkin spice latte," he reminded her.

Ignoring her friends' protests, Eva's slender hand curled around the handle.

Franklin smiled. "I'll just go lock the door…"

EVERY LITTLE THING

This was a fun one – it grew out of a challenge in my writing group to write a story where a dish sponge played an important role. It's very important to keep your tools clean, after all.

"How do you attach memories to a dish sponge?"

Moira couldn't answer Kenneth's question. She just shook her head wordlessly as sobs trickled out from her compressed lips, making that horrible snuffling noise she made when she was trying not to cry. Tears leaked down her face despite her efforts.

Kenneth sighed and with exaggerated care he placed the bright blue dish sponge back into the mouth of the ceramic frog perched on the edge of the sink.

"Honestly, Moira, if you can't let some things go, we're going to be here all bloody night." Kenneth ran his hand through his thick shock of black hair and looked down at his twin sister.

"I know," she sniffled. "But I can't, Kenneth. I just can't. Everything reminds me of Burt. Every little thing."

Kenneth gestured to the clutter that surrounded them. "All of this reminds you of Burt?" he demanded, "Right down to that tatty, filthy dish sponge? What about that almost empty bottle of Palmolive? Does that remind you of your missing husband too?" He yearned to point out that this was her third failed marriage, but that would just invite more waterworks and slow them down more.

Moria's bottom lip started to tremble uncontrollaby again, and Kenneth muttered, "For pity's sake."

"I can't help it," Moira blurted, "You know how I am Kenneth, how helpless I am. Oh Kenneth, what will I do without him? He wasn't very nice, and he liked to spend our money on beer, and I think he might have had something going with his secretary. But having him here was better than being alone. You know I can't be alone, Kenneth. I just can't."

Kenneth knew it all too well. His entire life he'd been taking care of Moira. Her most recent marriage had been his salvation. It was a shame that barely four years in Burt had decided he'd had enough and had flown the coop. He'd lasted longer than Curtis and Liam, neither of whom had made the two-year mark.

Moira had heralded the loss in typical Moira fashion – a tearful middle of the night phone call to the only family she had left in the world – her brother Kenneth. No matter that it was only five days until Christmas. And in typical brother Kenneth fashion, here he was two days later, rented U-Haul in the driveway, ready to ferry Moira and her belongings back to his home in Thunder Bay.

But she had to get rid of a few things. As many as he could convince her to part with. She was going from a two-bedroom bungalow to a single room in Kenneth's home. His wife was going to be mad enough about having Moira living with them again – she would go ballistic if there was a glut of Moira's stuff to contend with.

Moira struggled to her feet from where she'd collapsed to the floor, overcome her despair at his callous suggestion that they dispose of a grungy old blue dish sponge. He eyed an almost empty bottle of olive oil, imagining her hysterics if he suggested they dispose of that.

She folded her arms around him.

"Thank you for coming to get me, Kenny," she whispered, "Are you sure Carol doesn't mind?"

Oh, Carol minded all right. His wife was not in favour of allowing her dependent and unstable sister-in-law to move in with them. And she was very angry at being left to finish the Christmas preparations while Kenneth was half-way across the province helping Moira. Kenneth figured he'd sort all that out later. Once he'd rescued Moira. Again. He would be in for months of cold shoulders and snide under the breath comments until Carol finally decided to forgive him. He couldn't think about that right now. Kenneth could only deal with one impossible woman at a time, and right now that woman was clinging to him, her shoulders bucking like she was about to start sobbing again.

"Okay, maybe we shouldn't have started with the kitchen," Kenneth suggested quickly, "Maybe somewhere less personal. What about the shed?"

"No!" Moira pulled away from him. "I mean... Burt's tools are out there, and I can't bear to look at them..."

Kenneth nodded. Anything to stave off more blubbering. "Well, where should we start?" Maybe she could offer another spot to begin packing her up for her move. Her house was quite small, and they were running out of options.

"Why don't I take you out for dinner?" she chirped. "We can figure out a plan of attack while we eat."

He agreed. Getting her out of the house would hopefully let her get some perspective on the issue.

"But nowhere that you and Burt used to go," he warned. The last thing he wanted was an uncomfortable scene in public while she bawled over a napkin dispenser or a plate of onion rings.

"Don't worry. Burt never took me anywhere. I think he was either too cheap or too ashamed of me."

Dinner was good. The two beers he had with dinner were even better. When they got home, there was no packing, just hot chocolate with generous dollops of peppermint schnapps and several rollicking games of Oh Snap!

Kenneth woke later that night with only dim memories

of the card games and then passing out. His head ached and his tongue felt thick and pasty with the aftermath of the schnapps.

Moira was nowhere to be seen. She was probably asleep. Or maybe she was huddled in the bedroom closet clutching Bert's discarded shoehorn to her chest and weeping. Either way, Kenneth was alone for the moment.

Kenneth stood up, swaying a bit. He looked out the living room window. The rented moving van hunkered down at the curb accusingly.

He was awake and there was no weepy Moira in the vicinity. Time to pack.

Kenneth knew she'd wake up if he started anywhere in the house, so he made his way to the shed, picking his away along the icy path that led to it.

The shed was dominated by a massive woodchipper. A large red bow was tied around the discharge spout together with a large gift tag. "Happy Early Christmas, Burt-Burt! Love, Moira-Bear!"

Kenneth circled it, looking at it from every angle and back to the narrow door that led out of the shed. He couldn't see any other way to get it out. He'd have to take it apart. He found Burt's toolbox and got to it.

He was very impressed by how clean the woodchipper was. He supposed that maybe Burt hadn't had a chance to use it before he did his midnight flit. Every inch of the machine gleamed, even more than if it had just come out of the box. It seemed to have been scrubbed. The scent of Palmolive was overpowering in spots as he methodically unscrewed parts and laid them aside.

As he worked and as he noticed the excessive, obsessive cleanliness of the woodchipper, he steadfastly and repeatedly pushed back the little disquieting thoughts that insisted on creeping back in.

When he finally had the whole thing pulled apart, a small

dark stain in the innermost workings completed the ugly picture. Maybe Moira wasn't as helpless as they thought she was. Maybe Burt hadn't left her at all. He wondered about Curtis and Liam. They'd both also done midnight flits. Kenneth wondered if large power tools had factored into those disappearances as well.

"I wish you hadn't found that." Moira sounded calm and collected. She watched from the open door. Cold air snuck into the room around them, another witness to the unspoken discovery.

"You missed a spot." It was all Kenneth could think of to say. He pointed it out, then stood numbly by while she went at it with sponge and Palmolive. Moira cleaned the offending spot very quicky and efficiently. Kenneth couldn't help but feel that this was something she may have done before. At least twice.

"So now what?" Moira asked him. They both regarded the now sparkling woodchipper.

Kenneth shrugged. "Let's pack you up," he said. "I'd like to be on the road by first light."

"What about that?" Moira nodded at the disassembled woodchipper.

"We'll pack it up." Kenneth had a hunch Carol was going to be difficult about this. And he had another hunch – that Moira knew a thing or two about dealing with difficult spouses…

CABIN FEVER

No Christmas collection is complete without a story about Krampus...

The shadows of the branches across her bed made Darla think of her room in the asylum.

Thinking of it made her homesick in a way she'd never felt about her actual home. She missed the squeak of white loafers against linoleum, the jingle of keys and the low-level buzz and thrum of the madness of others.

Here, in a cabin in some woods far away from that sterile comfort, she might as well have been on Mars.

Mike snorted in his sleep and shifted. Darla held her breath and willed herself to stillness. She kept her arms rigid at her sides, fearful lest he touch her. She didn't want him to. She wanted him to.

Her own internal contradictions kept her awake as they always had, ever since she was ten and had her first "incident". "Incident". That lovely little euphemism that her mother always accompanied with just the slightest well-bred lift of one corner of her upper lip.

Nothing ever kept Mike awake. Not even tonight, his wife's first night home from the place she'd been for the past three months. Darla would have thought he'd be awake alongside her, or at least rouse himself periodically to check in on her. They'd been in bed for four hours and he'd been fast asleep for three hours and fifty-five minutes of them.

She should try to sleep. Her parents were coming tomorrow to spend the time until Christmas with them and she was going to need all her strength to get through the next three weeks.

She couldn't sleep. She turned to her side, staring out at the shadowy room. The closet door stood slightly ajar. She couldn't bear half-open doors. Anything could hide behind them. She was afraid to get out and go the closet. What if there was something (with claws) under her bed?

A shadow flitted across the gap. Darla shrank back, momentarily forgetting her antipathy about being touched by her husband. It almost felt comforting to have the shelter of his body against her. His hand moved to rest heavily on her hip, and she flinched away from its oppressive familiarity.

Darla had to get out of this bed. She couldn't bear it for one more second. She quietly sat up, keeping her gaze fixed on the closet. Her heart pounded so loudly she was surprised Mike couldn't hear it over his raspy snores.

He sensed her change in position and mumbled something that sounded like a question.

"Going to the bathroom," she lied. He muttered and settled back down into whatever dreams he was having.

She kept her slippers and bathrobe close at hand and donned them both quickly. The cabin was solidly built, but the floors were greedy leeches when bare feet were on the menu. She kept an eye on the narrow gap of the closet door and edged her way to the door leading to the hall.

Once the door was closed behind her, she could breathe easier. She didn't have to use the facilities, but she put on the show – going in and lowering her bottoms. The toilet seat was a cold surprise that managed to shock a dribble from her.

After washing her hands, she went for a prowl through the house. She checked the children, relieved to find them all fast asleep – six-year-old Hannah, four-year old Frederick, and six-month old Tilda – the reason for her most recent stay at

Sunnyview Rest Home. Post partum was a bitch.

She was tired but there was no way she was going back to the room with the closet. She paused to check on the room she'd prepared for her parents. The bed was neat, and towels were laid out on the dresser.

This room had no closet.

It was perfect. She didn't know what she'd do tomorrow night, but for tonight, Darla had the answer.

• •

"You want to what?" Mike kept his expression carefully bland. Darla knew it was one of the "strategies" her doctors would have suggested that Mike "employ to facilitate a successful return to her previous competencies".

"I want to sleep in the second bedroom. We can let my parents have our room."

She could read the objection in Mikes eyes, his dismay at the prospect of having to move their belongings to a new room, the looming nights on a mattress that had seen better days. There was a reason why it had been relegated to the guest room once they'd bought the very expensive orthopaedic mattress that graced their bed in the master bedroom.

Mike did not voice the anticipated objection. Instead, he gave her a smile that was too brittle and too brief. "Sure, why not? It'll be like roughing it." He turned to the shelf over the sink. "Now let's get your pills…" He picked up the bottle and the pills (teeth) inside it rattled.

Her hand trembled as she held it out for him to drop her morning pills (teeth) into it. She was relieved to see the three white capsules and not the other things. The things she saw if she wasn't vigilant about medication, rest, and nutrition. The three pillars that formed the foundation of mental health. At least according to her doctors. She swallowed them with a glass of water.

"What do you want for breakfast?" he asked.

"Just coffee."

A brief wrinkle knit his brows together. "You need more than that."

Two bodies hurtled into the kitchen. "Daddy!"

Mike stooped down to gather Hannah and Frederick in for morning hugs and then gently urged them to do the same for their mother. They approached her reluctantly. They had visited her in the hospital only a few times and three months was a long time for them to go without seeing her.

Darla squatted down to their level, holding her arms open wide so they could come into her embrace. They folded themselves into the hug, and their little hands (claws) patted and stroked her cheeks and hair. She allowed herself the luxury of smelling them – the baby powdered innocent freshness of their skin.

"So, I was thinking pancakes for breakfast and then we go sledding while we wait for Oma and Opa." Squeals of joy greeted Mike's suggestion. "You can rest while we're outside," he added to Darla.

"No, I think I'd like to come outside," she answered. He seemed surprised. "The only way to get back to normal is to do normal things," she reminded him. It was another of the doctors' mantras.

Darla managed to eat a pancake and then she got to feed Tilda while Mike cleaned up after breakfast. It felt good to hold her baby in her arms again.

They suited everyone up and trooped outside. They had a wee sled for the baby and Darla settled her in it and began dragging her back and forth in the yard while Mike and the two older kids went whooping down the small hill by the house.

It was better outside. It was clean and bright and fresh

and white – just like being in the hospital again. If she closed her eyes and inhaled deeply, she could pretend the faint scent of pine coming from the dark forest at the rear of their property was the miasma of industrial disinfectant that hung over the ward like cheap perfume at a high school dance.

"Mommy watch!" Hannah's shriek pried her eyelids open, and she turned to watch her daughter hurtle down the hill on her snow saucer. She tumbled off at the end of the run, but jumped back up, laughing, and dusting clumps of snow off her purple snow suit. "Mommy, did you watch? Did you see me?"

"Yes, darling, I saw you. You were going so fast!"

In the small sled Tilda blatted noisily and then whimpered. Darla scooped her up to rest her against her hip in the time-worn sway/jiggle that all mothers instinctively adopted to soothe a fussy baby.

The woods seemed to have crept closer while Darla wasn't looking. Their dark shadows yawed hungrily, covering half of the field that separated their house from the murky gaps (mouths) and stalwart trees (ribs) of the forest.

A shivery finger of fear trailed up her spine and she pulled Tilda closer to her. The baby squawked, drawing Mikes attention.

"Is everything all right?" he called out. He had his sled in one hand and was holding Hannah's mittened hand in the other. Trust Mike to be the perfect father and husband - even way out here in the wilderness where the only audience was their children and whatever was lurking in the woods.

"Fine." Her cold cheeks creased with her superficial smile. "I think Tilda needs a change and we're getting cold. We're going to head inside."

"We'll come too." Mike stepped forward, ignoring the dismayed cries of his two older children, who wanted to stay outside and continue sledding.

"No, no, it's all right. I think we can manage…"

The distant slam of a car door removed any need for reply. Her parents had arrived.

• •

"I still don't think I understand…" Barbara's face wore an expression of polite inquiry.

"Darla wants you to have the main bedroom." Mike grinned in an effort to add lightness to the undercurrent of their conversation. His unstable wife was making unreasonable demands and they all had to go along to stave off another mental breakdown.

"But… why?" Barbara looked at her daughter.

"Barb, just do it." Karl's voice was a solid rumble. He looked at his wife. "If Darla wants to do it, we should go along with it." He grinned and put a hand on his back. "It's better this way. The mattress in that spare room is a killer."

Mike nodded his acknowledgement tightly. "It is at that. You guys get caught up. I'll get the bags and move our things to the other room." He gestured to the kitchen. "There's coffee if you'd like some."

"I can get it." Darla started to stand up. Anything to be helpful, to stop the looks of loving pity her mother was giving her.

"Stay and visit with your mom." Karl was already on the move to the kitchen. "I'll get the coffee."

Alone with her mother, Darla had no other choice but to face her.

"Well now." Her mother's voice was too bright, too cheerful. Too everything. "How are you doing?" Her head tilted in concern as she leaned closer, reaching over to rest her hand (claw) on Darla's knee. "How are you feeling?"

"I'm fine." Darla swallowed her urge to fling her mother's hand (claw) away from her.

"Mike did such an amazing job with the kids and house," Barbara commented. "You're so lucky to have him."

Darla nodded and was spared the necessity of having to comment by the arrival of her father with a tray of steaming mugs of coffee. By the time she'd doctored hers up, Mike had returned from fetching the bags. Darla didn't have to take part in the conversation. She could sit and sip her coffee and nod while the tides of words from her loved ones eddied and flowed around the rocky depths of her madness.

"Opa!" Hannah and Frederick hurtled into the room and up into their grandfather's lap.

"Who's ready for Krampus?"

Mike shook his head. "Karl… we don't do Krampus…" He tilted his head, the point of his chin indicating Darla as plainly as if he'd leapt to his feet and pointed an accusing finger at her.

"It's all right, Mike," Darla assured her husband. "I can handle it."

Mike continued to watch her warily.

"It's part of our heritage, Mike," Karl rumbled, "And if Darla says she's okay with it…" Karl dismissed any further discussion on the topic by starting to growl at the children, who shrieked in laughter and ran from the room. He scurried after them, growling louder and threatening to bite and scratch them.

Darla remembered Karl playing in a similar way with her and her sister Dot. She wondered if that was where her issues with teeth and nails (claws) started – or were the roots much deeper and darker, to those nocturnal visits from her grandfather when they spent the night at his house? She'd never talked about it with anyone, not even her doctors at the hospital. Her Opa had told her not to – that it was their little secret (curse). She never even knew if Dot had the same secret (curse). They'd never talked about it. Dot had died (escaped) in a car accident years ago.

Darla was suddenly exhausted. She didn't know if it was thinking about Dot, listening to her father chase her children around the house, trying to converse with her mother and Mike or just her pills. She needed to rest. She was supposed to rest when she needed it. Everyone said.

"I have to go rest now." She delivered the statement abruptly, interrupting whatever anecdote about the children Mike was relating.

He immediately stood up. "Do you want some help?"

"No. I can do it myself." It was amusing to hear herself echo the common lament of her two eldest children in their ongoing quest for autonomy.

Mike's gaze drifted to the clock on the mantle above the fireplace. "It's almost time for your pills."

"I'll get them." Barbara was halfway to her feet.

"Mom, I can do this myself." Before Barb could continue, Darla hurried past her and into the kitchen. She shook the bottle ostentatiously, making the pills (teeth) rattle loud enough so her loving family (captors) could hear. She turned the tap on, letting the water run so it would be cool to wash down her medicine (poison). She spilled the pills (teeth) into her open palm, counted out the three she was supposed to take and carefully sliding the overflow back into the amber bottle. Mike kept a close eye on these things – pills, bills, his insane wife. She tipped her open palm to the side. Oops – three pills down the drain. She drank a glass of water, leaving the dirty glass on the side of the sink.

Satisfied with her deception (salvation), Darla went into the guest bedroom to lie down.

• •

"—not healthy."

Darla awoke in a dark room. She didn't know what time or day it was, only that she'd had a decent sleep for the first time since she'd left the hospital (haven). The pills always imposed an artificial kind of fatigue on her, a determination that she would sleep whether she was ready to or not. It felt good to be the one driving the slumber train for a change. Darla wanted to expand that independence, be back in control of herself, her life, and her narrative. She didn't want to be "poor insane Darla" any longer. Poor Darla who saw things that weren't there. Who insisted that pills were teeth – who would ever think such a crazy thing?

She could hear the low murmur of voices of her family in the other room. There was a muted clink and the scent of roasting meat. They were getting dinner ready.

Darla slid her feet into her slippers and scuffed her way silently to the door of her bedroom. She eased the door open, ever acutely aware that eavesdroppers very rarely heard good of themselves.

"I think she's recovering well." Mike, ever the staunch husband, always in Darla's corner sounded as though he were exasperated. An afternoon spent with Darla's parents could have that effect on even the most patient of people.

"She seemed thin." Barbara was fussing as usual over Darla's appearance. Appearances were everything. "I've added a little extra butter to the sauce. Hopefully it helps her fatten up a bit."

"She'll be fine." Karl spoke dismissively. "She's always been a strong kid."

"She isn't a kid," Barbara pointed out acidly. "She is a grown woman with responsibilities – a home, a husband, our three adorable grandchildren. There just isn't room for her malingering any longer. Mike, you must insist she – "

"She what?" Darla couldn't stand listening to them any longer and she popped around the corner. "What do you think Mike should insist I do, Mother?"

"Why get more rest and take your pills of course…" Barbara

stopped stirring the pot of sauce for one second to come and kiss Darla's cheek. "How was your nap, darling?"

"I was just about to come and get you," Mike said. "Dinner's ready."

"You slept the day away." Barbara could make any innocent statement resonate like an accusation.

"It's the pills." Mike came to her defence. "They make her sleepy."

"Here." Barbara pushed a bowl of mashed potatoes into her hands. "Carry this to the table and we'll bring the rest in."

There were only four places set for dinner. "Where are the children?" Darla tried to keep her question at a reasonable tone and not give in to the bright edges of panic that were fraying at her. "Why are there no places set for them?"

"We fed them earlier." Barbara was on her heels, bearing a basket of rolls. "They're in bed."

"I don't know if they're asleep yet," Karl commented as he added a plate of carved beef to the table. "They're pretty excited about Krampus."

"We don't have anything…" Darla hadn't thought of it in the hospital, and it wasn't part of Mike's family experience. He wouldn't have thought of it or known what to get.

"We have everything," Barbara assured her daughter. "We knew you wouldn't have time." Another of her famous accusatory statements.

"We brought oranges and chocolate," Karl interjected. "And a new sleeper for the baby."

"She's too young for chocolate," Mike pointed out.

"She's too young to worry about Krampus," Karl added. "He only goes after wicked boys and girls. The baby is too young to be wicked."

"You'll be singing a different song when she wakes the household up at two in the morning for her feeding," Mike joked. "Now, let's eat and we can put the stuff out for the kids later."

Darla took her spot at the table. Mike had already set the little amber bottle at her place, along with a water glass. The others had wine. Darla had pharmaceuticals. She shook three pills (teeth) out of the bottle and into the palm of her hand. There was no convenient sink nearby to "accidentally" drop them into. She put them into her mouth and used her tongue to push them into a little corner between her cheek and jaw. The water she drank washed harmlessly by, leaving them in place.

Her secret left a bitter, chemical taste in her mouth. She knew she was absorbing tiny amounts of the pills into her bloodstream as the meal went on, but it was far preferable to allowing the full dose to invade her body. She ensured they saw her eat several bites of food and finish off her water before she excused herself briefly to the washroom.

The pills (teeth) sank through the pale yellow of her urine to rest on the bottom of the bowl until a push of the lever washed them out into the hungry septic tank that squatted under the earthy meat of their back yard. She washed her hands and returned to the table.

After supper they laid out the treats for the children and then played euchre. Darla had never been a fan of it and hadn't really played it since her university days. In the hospital she'd rediscovered it and played for hours on end with her fellow patients (family). She was the only one not surprised when she won.

The big meal and mountain air did everyone in and they retired early. Mike only muttered for a few minutes about how uncomfortable the spare bedroom bed was and then he sank into sleep.

Darla lay awake. She'd expected that after her big nap and with not taking her pills that she might not be able to fall asleep right away. She relished the idea of being awake and alone, of not having to watch her words and actions lest she be targeted as mad again.

The night, once her adversary, was now her friend. She lay on her back and watched the waving limbs of the shadow trees on the ceiling. They were friendly and not scary at all.

Until the scratching started.

The slow unwavering echo drove Darla into the safety (trap) of the blankets. She pulled them up over her head, burrowing down. She shifted herself backwards until she was in the shelter of Mike's slumber.

"Too hot. Darla…" he protested in a sleep-sodden whine and turned his back to her, using his hip to push her away from him. She was on her own with the not-so-friendly-now trees and the slow scratching sounds that were either the inside of her skull or the outside of the cabin. Or maybe both.

She emerged from the tangle of sheets and bedding, relieved that there was no closet in this room, no gap in the darkness that could harbour any number of ills.

She didn't have a closet in her room. But there were other closets, other opportunities for evil to hide. Her children.

Her slippers pit patted through the house as she sought a means of defence. She contemplated the pill bottle on the counter. If she took them all, she'd finally rest. And wake up back at the hospital. Was that what she wanted? Well, was it?

She could almost hear Barbara's arch voice demanding answers to the question. In a word, yes. Or maybe. Maybe it was what Darla wanted.

The scratching was getting louder, and she could hear whispers underneath it. No words, just sibilant hisses and groans that were far worse.

One of her hands closed around the pill bottle. The other

one closed around the largest carving knife sitting in the drying rack. A quick fumble through the tool drawer located the pliers. She slid all her tools into the pocket of her robe. One way or another the scratching was going to stop.

The house watched her moving through oppressive and silent darkness as she made her patrol. The front hall closet was clear as was the linen closet outside the bathroom.

The scratching got louder as she reached the children's room. She knew it would. She knew exactly where it was, what it wanted. What it needed.

Twin chests in twin beds rose and fell in perfect unison. An infant in a crib cooed peacefully in her sleep, fist wedged into her mouth.

And in the closet, the scratching grew louder. It was eager.

"Me or them. Is that it?" She stuck her hands into the deep pockets of her robe, fingering the tools she'd brought with her.

It didn't answer. It didn't have to. She knew what it wanted, what it needed. What she needed.

****

"Mommy was eating jam in our closet," Frederick announced as he came into his father's room. "Silly Mommy."

"What?" Mike was half awake, still muzzy in the head. He reached out with his hand to find Darla's side of the bed empty and cold.

"She has jam all over her face and down her front and she's sleeping," Frederick announced, "I think she pooed a bit too. It's stinky. Can I sleep in your bed?"

"Where are your sisters?" Mike sat upright, swinging his legs over the side of the bed, toes searching for slippers.

"Still sleeping." Frederick slid under the covers, nestling down in the space vacated by Mike. "Nice and comfy, Daddy."

Mike prayed under his breath, hurrying to his children's room to discover the inevitable. He'd known for years they were going to end up here – he had hoped it wouldn't be this soon.

He checked the girls first. Darla would never... and she hadn't. Both Hannah and Tilda were still asleep. Still safe. He turned to the closet, remembering what Frederick had said.

"Darla..." One of her bare feet poked out of the closet into the room, toes flexed as if she were going to wiggle them at him playfully. He looked far enough into the closet to see the ugly tableau. Darla's poor tortured body and the tools she'd used. "Oh... Darla..."

The knife for her neck.

The pliers for her jaws.

The empty pill bottle for insurance.

Two bloody mouths gaping in tandem – one above and one below her finely sculpted chin.

The spray of teeth scattered across the wooden floor.

CHRISTMAS EVE

The day before Christmas is in some ways and for some people just as important as Christmas Day. Our family has a laundry list of traditions we engage in on Christmas Eve. I won't go into detail here. Suffice it to say that for our household, Christmas Eve is almost a holiday unto itself.

When my kids were small, I used to read them the same story every year – "10 Timid Ghosts". Even on Christmas Eve, there had to be a touch of the spooky amidst our celebrations.

On Christmas Eve, the excitement around Christmas reaches fever pitch. Children find it hard to sleep. So do parents, but for a very different reason. *How* many pieces does that doll house have? Where are we supposed to find eight AAA batteries at ten o'clock at night?

Some people spend Christmas Eve in quiet reflection, embracing the spirituality of the season. They may go to church, or they may just spend it alone with their thoughts.

A lot of people head out into the fray of last-minute shoppers, trying to get everything on their list before the stores close at six pm.

And the people in the following stories are all having a very bad Christmas Eve…

PETER PORTER AND THE MAGICAL WISHING SQUID

When my brother and I were small, our parents took us to a restaurant for lunch on Christmas Eve in an attempt to curb our pre-Christmas shenanigans. It's a practice I have continued with my own children. However, not everyone you see at a restaurant on Christmas Eve is there to celebrate the season...

Peter didn't want to go to this restaurant - and then he saw the squid.

It was coiled in the corner of the aquarium that separated the dining room from the entrance. In a tank of silvery minnows, golden carp and neon-coloured tetras, the grey lumpy squid should have faded into the background.

It captured Peter's attention. He eased over, the better to observe the squid's large bulbous eyes and gently waving tentacles. It looked like it was waving at him, a jaunty "hello Peter!"

He heard Jack (call-me-Jack-or-you-can-call-me-Dad-if-you-want) telling the hostess there'd be five of them for supper. Jack, Peter's mom and sister and Jack's mom.

The squid waved at him again. One opalescent eye opened and closed slowly. It was winking at him.

Peter closed his eyes, rubbing at the corners with his

knuckles hard enough that his mother asked if he was tired. Peter shook his head and opened his eyes as wide as he could to negate her assumption.

If Jack-call-me-Jack hadn't been here, his mother would have teased him that he was waiting for Santa. It was Christmas Eve. Santa would be coming.

Not to Peter. Jack didn't celebrate Christmas, so Peter's mother didn't celebrate Christmas anymore, which meant Peter and Penny couldn't have Christmas. Jack was an A-THE-ist, whatever that was.

It wasn't fair.

If Peter's dad had still been around, they could've had Christmas. Even after they'd moved away from Dad's house, they'd had Christmas. It hadn't been much of one. Peter's mother had spent a lot of it crying and apologizing for them still being in the shelter. It had been nice there. They'd gotten candy and some toys from some church that felt bad they were in the shelter.

Then Jack-call-me-Jack had come along. Suddenly Mom wasn't crying all the time. She smiled lots and even wore the perfume that made her smell like cupcakes.

"Stop scowling Peter." Mom bent down so her eyes were on a level with Peter's. "It's very nice of Jack to take us out for dinner."

"I don't want to eat here."

"But this was always your favourite restaurant. They have dino nuggets." Mom glanced over her shoulder. Jack-call-me-Jack was following the waitress to their table. Penny's hand was tucked trustingly into his. Traitor.

"It was my favourite when we used to come here with Dad." Peter felt a spike of mean gratification at the way his mother flinched at the mention of his father. "Now I hate it." Over his mother's shoulder the squid squinted warningly at Peter. "I don't want to eat here. And I want Santa to come." He had a niggling suspicion that at thirteen years old, he was probably too old for Santa. His Mom was always telling people that Peter was "special" and "a bit young for his age". He supposed that meant he could still whine for Santa like he was seven – the same age as Penny.

"Peter we've been over this. Jack's family doesn't celebrate Christmas. We must be sensitive to that."

Peter crossed his arms defiantly. "I want Santa. I want presents. I don't want to eat here." His lower lip trembled.

"Peter…" His mother's arms beckoned him in for a hug. "Jack has been very generous. He's given us lots of presents. We don't need more presents tomorrow. You and Penny and I can have our own little celebration another time. Please. This is very important." She was using her serious voice. Over her shoulder the squid nodded encouragingly.

Peter grudgingly allowed his mother to hug him. He closed his eyes for a minute, savouring the scent of cupcakes and the soapy smell of her happiness. He could do this.

Peter took his seat beside Penny with his mother on his other side and ignored the looks from Jack's mother. He'd overheard her asking Jack, "Is that boy some kind of retard?" It made him mad. He knew the "r" word was a bad one. It made his mother sad. His dad used to get mad whenever he heard it.

The waitress bustled over. "Welcome to Lotus Blossom." She had a nice smile and she smelled like French fries. Peter liked her already.

"Lotus Blossom." Penny giggled. "Mommy calls Peter her little Lotus Blossom sometimes…"

Peter blushed. That was a secret name between him and his mom. He didn't want anyone else hearing it.

Mom ruffled his hair. "That's what I used to call Peter when he was a baby. My little lotus blossom…"

"Mo-o-o-o-m…" Peter dragged the word out into seven

embarrassed syllables.

The waitress didn't dwell on the nickname. She took their drink orders and left them to study the menus. Peter didn't need to study the menu. He wanted dino nuggets and French fries.

The waitress returned with their drinks. "Does anyone have any questions or are you ready to order?"

"What's the squid's name?" Peter blurted. His mother shushed him. Jack and Jack's mom both scowled at him.

The waitress wasn't fazed. "I don't think he has one. Should we give him a name?"

"Yes. Albert."

The waitress nodded. "That's a good name." She waved her pen towards the aquarium. "I dub thee Sir Albert of Tanklovia. Any other questions?"

"Is he magic?" He had to be magic, the way he kept winking and nodding at Peter. The way he seemed to know what Peter was thinking.

The waitress shook her head. "No." Her voice sharpened. Everyone's voice got like that when Peter started asking them questions. It made him sad. Everyone except Mommy got angry and impatient when they had to keep talking to Peter. "He's just a regular old squid. Now does anyone have any questions about the food?"

Jack-call-me-Jack hurried to order their food before Peter could come up with any other questions. At least he remembered to order dino nuggets.

They'd have to wait for their food. Peter hated waiting for food. "Mom, can I go to the bathroom?" he whispered.

His mother moved to push her chair back to accompany him.

"I can go by myself," he asserted. "I remember the way."

"If you're sure…"

He nodded. "I want to be independent." He wasn't entirely sure what that word meant, only that Miss Purcell, his assistant at school kept telling him he had to try to be more independent.

The tank was on the way to the rest rooms. He had a very important mission, otherwise he'd have to stop and wonder why they were called "rest" rooms when there weren't any beds in them.

Albert waved and winked at Peter. "I know you're magic." Peter bent low to whisper through the glass. "I want to have Christmas again. Like when Daddy lived us. Without shouting." He hated it when Daddy shouted at Mommy. He and Penny would hide in his closet until the shouting stopped. It made Mommy sad. He didn't like it when Mommy was sad. "Can you please make it Christmas again? And maybe make Mommy be happy all the time. Not just when she's with Jack-call-me-Jack."

Albert communicated with waves and winks and taps on the glass. Peter understood. Albert was going to grant him his wish. Peter straightened up and saw Jack at the top of the stairs.

Jack was heading downstairs to the bathroom. He'd find out Peter wasn't in the bathroom. Peter would get in trouble if Jack found out he wasn't in the bathroom. Mommy didn't like it when Peter lied. It made her sad. Peter had to keep Jack from finding out he wasn't in the bathroom.

Peter barreled across the floor. His shoulder connected solidly with Jack's bum, heaving him forward and sending him in a mess of snaps and screams down the tile and steel steps.

Peter clapped his hands over his ears. He didn't like loud noises. When the snaps and screams stopped, Peter took his hands away from his ears. The last sound Jack made was a kind of gurgling moan and then it was silent. Quiet was good. Peter liked it when it was quiet.

Peter made his way back to the dining room. He wrung his hands together, acting as though he'd washed and dried them.

Mommy was always asking him if he'd washed his hands. Peter was very happy to see that his food had arrived. He sat down and started dolloping the ketchup in artful smears around the plate.

"Peter, what did you do?" his mother demanded.

She was already half out of her seat, starting towards the stairs where the thuds and shouts and gurgling noises had diminished to wonderful silence. Peter swirled the first dino through the ketchupy drift.

He gave her a wide smile, red dribbling down his chin. "I saved Christmas."

THE HOLLY AND THE IVY

A sweet tale of holiday revenge for your entertainment...

A Mardi Gras themed party on Christmas Eve was the dumbest thing Dan Fairchild had ever seen. Well, second dumbest he amended as he caught sight of their hostess. She sashayed around the room bearing a tray of canapes, layers of bead necklaces draped over her scantily clad body. Holly Playford was a junior secretary at his accounting firm. "Not bright" was an understatement of her mental acuity but she more than made up for it with her other many and bountiful assets.

The beard that went with his Santa suit was itchy. He pulled it aside to take another drink of his cocktail. He didn't know what was in it exactly, but it was blue, frothy, and fruity and it packed a hell of a punch. He was on his third. He should probably slow it down if he was going to have a chance with Holly. He wanted a chance with Holly. He wouldn't be wearing this stupid Santa suit otherwise. He'd overheard her confide in one of the other secretaries that she had a "thing" for Jolly Old Saint Nick and his jolly little ---

"Hey!" Dan blurted as he was jostled from behind. His cocktail slopped up over his fingers.

"Sorry, dude," the other man apologized. "Just going to get my coat."

"Yeah, yeah." Dan stepped out of his way.

"Oh, my goodness, Mister Fairchild." Holly was suddenly

there with a napkin. "Here, let me help." She began to enthusiastically blot at a dry area of the Santa suit that was located very south of where the spill had occurred.

"Um. Holly. The drink didn't get me there." But feel free to keep rubbing, he silently added. "And you can call me Dan. Or Santa if you'd rather..." He chuckled.

Holly straightened up and gave him a dazzling smile. "Let's get you another Blue Tuesday. Come on."

He followed her through the thinning crowd, admiring her curves and her bouncing waves of auburn hair. She hummed along with the brassy big band blaring from her stereo.

She handed him a fresh drink and guided him to an empty spot on the sofa. "Sit down. Enjoy your drink."

Enjoy it he did, followed by two more ferried his way by the doting Holly.

By the time the last party guest had left, he was half-reclining on the couch. His head lolled back against the headrest. His Santa coat was mostly undone to reveal a slice of his white undershirt.

Holly turned off the stereo, silencing the jazzy cheerfulness of the big bang era. The apartment was suddenly, heavily silent. He'd never understood the term "deafening silence" until now.

"I better... I should... I go..." he slurred, struggling against the sudden lethargy seeping into his limbs. He fought to sit up.

Holly placed a hand on his chest, pushing him back down.

"You're not going anywhere," she said. The ominous words were at odds with the lilting giggle in her breathy voice.

"I—" Dan knew he should say words, but he couldn't think of any.

"Oh please. Stay. We're going to have so much fun..." The words sounded playful, but her tone of voice was threatening.

The sound of duct tape being torn from the roll echoed through the silent apartment. He flinched at the coarse ripping sound and missed the hubbub of the stereo.

While he pondered the silence, Holly quickly wrapped the duct tape twice around his wrists, binding them together. Dan was vaguely aware that he should be alarmed, but this was kind of exciting. It reminded him of some of the naughty antics he'd gotten up to when he was a horny college student tearing up the streets of Oshawa.

Holly climbed up on the couch. Her knees bracketed his splayed thighs. Her slim fingers nimbly undid the buttons of his Santa pants. He tried to murmur encouraging words, but all his slackening facial muscles could manage was a lopsided leer and a slobbery sigh.

Holly called, "You can come out now."

The door to what Dan had presumed was Holly's bedroom opened and out came a copy of Holly – right down to the same kinky little elf outfit.

"This is Ivy," Holly said.

"Hey Dan," Ivy greeted him, "Remember us? Oh right. You don't know us."

"But we know you…" Holly added. She'd left her perch straddling Dan on the couch and was rummaging through drawers in the kitchen.

"You changed our lives," Ivy explained, "Twenty years ago tonight."

Dan struggled against the tape as hard as he was struggling to remember. There was something about this night. Something had happened on a Christmas Eve a very long time ago. Something that his parents had paid a lot of money to have him and everyone else involved forget.

"It was Christmas Eve. You had a part-time job as a mall

Santa. Just something to pick up some extra cash. Get nice presents for Dan Junior and baby Mya. Maybe something nice for your mistress so she wouldn't blow the whistle."

His mistress. Dan paused to think warm thoughts of Michelle, his first mistress and her warm thighs and welcoming heart. He hadn't thought of her in years. Good times.

"Noel also had a part time job," Holly picked up the narrative from her double. "She was one of your elves. She was young. So young."

Holly had her hands behind her back as she came back around the couch to stand beside Ivy. Dan stared at the two young women. There was an air of menace in the room looming large and he was struggling hard to understand through the fog in his brain, thanks to too many Blue Tuesdays.

"She had a lot of responsibilities for someone so young," Ivy continued. "Twin girls. Us. And that night was our second birthday. She wanted to be home from work in time for our party."

"But she was late. Very late. Because of you." Holly leaned closer and Dan saw the resemblance to Noel. He hadn't thought of her in years.

"She – I – we…" Dan wished his brain and mouth would co-operate. He wondered what had been in those drinks Holly had been pouring so freely.

"It's a story so trite that it's almost boring," Ivy continued. "A cold night… a pretty young girl…" Her hand settled on Dan's crotch, and she gave him a friendly squeeze. His brain and tongue might be dysfunctional, but part of him was ready to respond. "A dashing young man… a ride home…"

"Oh, we know what your story was," Holly glared at him. "You said it was consensual. You said she was lying."

"You said a lot of things, didn't you, Danny?" Ivy purred. Her hand tightened and his flesh responded.

"And in the end because you were from a good family and she wasn't and you had a full-time day job and she didn't, everyone believed you." Holly shook her head, her full lips twisting into a disgusted sneer. "And I'm sure the fact that your dad was golf buddies with the chief of police and the Crown attorney had no effect on her case, did it?"

"She tried," Ivy continued, "She really did. But after the lies you told, nobody trusted her. You made them believe she was a liar, a thief, a drug addict. Nobody gave her a chance. She couldn't get a job, couldn't keep a home… couldn't keep us."

"We were in foster care by Easter," Holly added, "And adopted to different homes by Thanksgiving."

"We never saw our mom or each other again." Ivy's hand worked hard at ensuring his body kept betraying him. "Until we found each other last year. And then we found her grave. Our Mom died before we were ten years old."

"It didn't take a lot of research to find you," Holly said, "You're pretty proud of yourself, aren't you, Dan? And you're still up to your old tricks. Seducing young women in precarious situations. You think you're so smart. Smarter than everyone else."

She'd completely lost the breathy little voice she'd previously had. Her voice was hard now. She took her hands out from behind her back. She passed the pliers to Ivy but held on to the butcher knife.

"We had to live without something we loved for twenty years. It's only fair you do the same. Now hold still. I'm afraid this might hurt a bit…"

BAGGAGE

Travel at any time can be aggravating. Christmas Eve travel is the worst...

Let me tell you about the last time I flew into Wayne County international airport. It's a freaky story and judging by the looks of those low hanging clouds, we're not taking off for quite a while yet.

Air travel's a bitch at the best of times. Traveling at the holidays is its own special kind of hell. You got family in Michigan? Me too. In Detroit. I know, it doesn't make sense that I'm not flying into Detroit. I'm flying into Kalamazoo, renting a car, and driving to Detroit. I know it sounds really convoluted but maybe after I tell you my story, you'll understand why it's gotta be like this. Hell, after you hear my story, maybe you'll give the Detroit airport a wide berth yourself.

I won't fly to Detroit. Not even as a layover. I could've booked a flight with only one stop on my way to Kalamazoo, but that stopover was in good old DTW. Nuh uh as my son would say. So, I stopped over in Charlotte, North Carolina for an hour and then spent a delightful two hours battling my way across Chicago airport to get to this flight. And now we're seat buddies. Cheers.

I don't like being in airports at night either. Not enough people around. I like it packed and full of bustle. I'm glad that this flight ends at three. By nightfall I'll be at my sister's house, drink in hand and curtains closed. Sure, it means I have to get up at the crack of dawn and hustle my ass to the airport in Jacksonville, but it's worth it to not be caught in the airport at night. You don't want that.

The last time I flew into Detroit was on Christmas Eve. My son was five then, so that's around seven years ago? My parents were alive then and I was flying back home to Michigan from Florida. I hated crowds then. I purposely took the latest flight out that I could. It would land me in Detroit at midnight. I didn't want the old man driving at night, so I told them I'd catch a cab at the airport. Uber wasn't really a thing yet.

I knew that by flying so late, there wouldn't be many people on the plane and probably no screaming kids at all. I was right. There was about a dozen of us on that plane, and I'm being generous and including the three sad flight attendants who'd drawn the short end of the stick to have to work on Christmas Eve.

The flight was okay, as flights go. It was what went down after in the airport that had me swearing off Wayne County airport. Hell, for the first two years, I wouldn't even fly. But driving home at Christmas ate up an extra five days and those were days I could've used elsewhere. So, I went back to flying, but not to Wayne County. Never again.

With so few people, I had an entire row to myself. It was glorious. Flipped the armrests up, stretched out sideways and napped my way from the sunbelt to the fanbelt. Little Motor City humour there.

You been to Wayne County? Yeah? So then you know what a slog it is to get to the baggage carousel. Up the escalator then down then down again. Literally one end of the airport to the other.

My flight's luggage was on carousel two – at the far end of the concourse. Of course. Just my freaking luck. Normally I'd fly with just my carry on if I was going home for a few days. You can get a lot into a small suitcase if you're creative. I could travel light back then because I used to keep some stuff at my folks' house. Things I didn't need in Florida. Winter boots and crap like that.

But it was Christmas. So, I had a suitcase full of presents for my parents and my sister and brother and their families. If I hadn't had the suitcase, I wouldn't have seen him, and I'd probably be blissfully flying in and out of DTW until this very day.

Or maybe not.

I'm not a superstitious man, nor do I believe in a lot of mystical crap apart from what I'm going to tell you. But I wonder sometimes if it wasn't predestined – if that creepy old dude was there only because I was there.

I saw him on my way to the baggage carousel. The bags weren't up yet, it was just whirling around and around while it waited for the baggage handlers to feed it. There were only a couple of us waiting for our bags and I think there was some conversation along the lines of how many baggage handlers does it take to move three suitcases and a set of skis. You know, the kind of gentle exasperation shared by strangers who are tired from traveling and eager to close out the last of their trip and hurry home.

He was off to the side, just where the carpet meets the tile. He was wearing a black suit. I remember thinking he was dressed awfully formally for airline travel. If the suit had been a bit fancier or in better condition, I almost might have thought he was a hired driver here to fetch the passengers, apart from the fact that he was sitting in a wheelchair. He was thin and hunched over – so much so that his knees were almost touching his earlobes. I didn't see an overcoat – just his suit and white shirt and black tie. The tie was just slightly askew, off kilter enough that my fingers twitched, wanting to reach out and straighten it. Touching him would have been a very bad idea.

He saw me looking at him.

"Hey." His voice was raspy, and whispery. It dropped little icicles down my spine. "I need help."

I didn't want to help him. I also didn't want to be the person who refused to help a feeble old man. That's bad karma for sure. I looked around to see if he could have been possibly addressing anyone else. The other few people in the vicinity were suddenly occupied with matters on the other side of the room, allowing them to turn their backs to my new friend and study the arrivals board intently. It suddenly seemed very important to all of them that they determine what time the plane from Denver would arrive.

"You. In the purple jacket."

The vitriol he put into the colour and description of my coat had me rethinking my wardrobe choice. I'd thought it jaunty and fashionable. Now it felt silly and juvenile.

I didn't know what to do. I didn't want to look at him. I didn't want to help him, but I still had my inbred need to not be "that guy" that was battling against my instincts.

Then I was saved by the bell. Literally. The guide lights flashed, and the bell rang to let us know our luggage was coming up from the belly of the plane.

My bag is never the first one off the plane and that night was no exception. The other four people in the area retrieved their bags first while I still stood at the edge of the carousel, ignoring the old man's attempts to get my attention. I kept my eyes fixed on the silvery scales of the belt as it trundled around the oblong track, waiting to see my hard sided Samsonite come sliding by.

It was just the old man and me now. He'd given up hissing to try to get my attention and we were both just watching the carousel in silence. A dark rectangle eased up the conveyor from the depths of the luggage area and tumbled onto the carousel. It wasn't my bag.

It was an older model. It didn't even have wheels on it. The side had several long scratches marring the surface. The handle looked like it had been chewed on and was ready to let go with the lightest of tugs. A tattered yellowed identification tag was looped around the handle, waving at me.

"Can you get my bag?" the old man wheezed.

"Were you on my flight?" I didn't remember seeing him among the passengers.

"'Course I was."

His bag was passing directly in front of me now and I let it go by. I didn't want to pick it up.

"Can you get it next time?" he demanded.

I ignored him and kept watch for my bag. Surely any second now it would emerge from the depths, and I could grab it. Let one of the skycaps help this old man. It was their job after all. Mine was just to get a cab, get home to my folks and get drunk on my dad's whiskey – in exactly that order.

"Hey, you… get my bag…" He wasn't giving up.

"What seat were you in?" I asked him.

"What?" He spat the word at me like something dark and grotty that was stuck in his ancient throat.

"I don't remember seeing you on my flight." Yeah, it was petty. But I was a younger man and a pettier man back then.

"Maybe you were too busy thinking about the waitress you banged Thursday night." He made a strangled sound that was somewhere between a wheeze and a cackle. I think he was trying to laugh.

I tried to tell myself it was a shot in the dark, just a random guess. But even now, I'm not sure.

Because I had been with a waitress the previous Thursday night. Those details aren't important, really. But yes, I had taken a waitress home from my local pub. I had spent some of the flight thinking about Brenda and planning to call her when the holidays were over.

I never did call her, by the way.

"Seat number," I repeated, trying to focus on that to quell the uneasy feelings I was having. Maybe two scotches during the flight hadn't been a great idea. Or maybe I should've had more.

"If you're going to get precious about it, my seat number was 28B. Does that make you happy? Here comes my suitcase again."

How could it be that his suitcase had made one full revolution of the conveyor and mine had yet to appear?

"Get my suitcase." The man's voice was sharper and colder. It made me flinch. "I answered your pointless question about my seat number. Get my damn suitcase, Junior."

I hadn't given him my name. Let alone the nickname my dad had for me when I was younger. The queasies were crawling from my stomach and up my spine.

I reached into my pocket for a tissue. I felt like I might be sick. My fingers closed around a piece of paper. I pulled it out. My boarding pass. Seat 28B.

The old man tried a different approach. He smiled. I wished he hadn't. The unholy grin seemed to stretch for forever, revealing a maw full of jagged and uneven yellowed teeth. His thin lips skinned back so that his pock marked gums were revealed in all their pulpy glory. The attempted jocularity of his lower face didn't match up with the hate and anger I saw in his dark eyes.

"If you want an incentive, I'll give you a nice tip. Enough to buy a fancy lawyer for a custody battle. Or enough to make sure the custody battle disappears into the swamps by Belle Chasse." He pronounced it flatly, "Bel Chase", but I knew what he was talking about.

My ex-wife had recently moved there, taking our son with her. She had filed for custody. One of the things I'd hoped to discuss with my parents over the Christmas break was the possibility of a small loan to hire a lawyer. It was too specific to be random.

"Who are you? Did Laura send you?" It didn't seem like her style to send someone to harass and annoy me, but since our divorce had turned nasty, I had discovered a few of her less admirable personality traits.

His smiled dimmed and his lips pursed. "Get my suitcase. I'll give you money. I'll even answer your questions." The smile returned, wider and creepier than ever. "But I don't think you'll like my answers very much…"

He peered past me. "It's coming back. Third time's a charm, monkeyboy." He hunched forward in his chair, eying me expectantly.

Another family nickname. But this one was from my grandma who had died when I was eight. Nobody else had ever called me that.

I didn't want to know how he knew about my grandma, my divorce, Brenda, or anything else. I didn't want to listen to him prattle on. And I sure as shit didn't want to touch that beat up suitcase with its ratty handle. Something told me that touching this man or anything belonging to him would be a spectacularly Bad Idea.

I did the only thing I could do. I booked it for the escalator to the taxi stand, ignoring his insults and orders. I took a cab home and told my family the airline had lost my suitcase. I endured their jibes Christmas morning when I didn't have presents for them and promised to make it up with astounding birthday gifts.

And the day after Boxing Day, I rented a car and drove back to Jacksonville. I made amends with Laura. We managed to work out custody arrangements without resorting to lawyers and ugliness. I never set foot in the Wayne County airport again.

Because he's still waiting for someone to fetch his suitcase.

THE 'S' IS FOR SANTA...

Not everyone celebrates Christmas Eve in a traditional manner.

"Santa..." Sam repeated it slowly.

"Yes." Jocelyn watched him warily, unsure of how he would react to her confession.

He shook his head, his dark hair flopping over one eye. If her hands were free, she'd have reached up to smooth it away from his hazel eyes.

"Your most shameful kink is... you want to do it with Santa Claus..." To his credit, the corner of his lip only quirked instead of fanning out into the full grin she was sure he was concealing.

"Not the actual Santa Claus," she assured him. "I mean, I know he's not real... but I just kind of get off on that scene... you know... he sees you when you're sleeping. And the whole naughty list thing..."

Sam rolled over on top of her, his knees straddling her narrow hips. His hands came to rest on the padded leather buckles that held her in spread eagle position on the bed.

"Why Jocelyn Wiseman..." he murmured throatily. "Are you a very bad girl..."

Even though moments ago she'd been spent from their extended play, she suddenly felt a slow spark that told her she could quite probably go again. It was the effect of his deep voice, the wicked glint in his eyes and his willingness to play out whatever fantasy she mentioned.

She bit her lip, looking up at him. "The absolute worst..." she whispered.

His fingers worked at the cuffs. She was disappointed when he released first one, then the other wrist and then her ankles.

Sam settled himself on the loveseat that was positioned with the best view of the bed and gestured to her to come to him. She crawled off the bed and up into his lap. He pulled the plush throw from the arm of the loveseat to surround her naked body with the soft warmth. Jocelyn snuggled into the depths of his arms. Aftercare was just as good as the play time – and just as important.

"Now..." He rubbed his hands slowly up and down her arms, caressing her through the blankets he had her bundled in. "Tell me about this Santa thing... how old were you when it started?"

"I think I've always had a thing for him..." She leaned her head on Sam's shoulder. "You know I love being watched. And the idea of being punished for being bad... that goes back a long way."

"So ... what should Santa punish you for?"

Jocelyn shivered at the gentle press of his lips in the crook of her neck. He was so tender and loving during aftercare.

"Everything..." she whispered.

His hand stopped moving and put gentle pressure on the crook of her elbow. The time for punishment was over – for now. The unyielding presence of his hand was her reminder that he could still start things back in motion again – starting with a swift spanking. She didn't want that. She didn't want to disrupt the wonderful lassitude that seeped through her body after a play session. It was only her naked honesty that would belay the sting of the strap.

"Be more specific." His voice was calm and unhurried as

it usually was during their play sessions. "What should Santa punish you for, Jocelyn?"

"I was a very bad child. I once locked my sister outside in the snow in her underwear. It was February. She got a very bad cold afterwards."

Sam chuckled and his hand resumed the slow caresses of her body. "I'd have liked to see that," he mused, "Maybe it's why Tina grew up to be such a cold bitch."

Jocelyn giggled. "Maybe…"

"What else?" He paused and his lips pursed as he contemplated. "Give me two more bad things you've done. Something as a teenager and something more recent… something that I don't know about…"

Jocelyn's lips parted as she prepared to deny any of her current sins. He halted her with his forefinger against her lower lip.

"Don't even try to deny it," he commanded. "You know you've done things and hidden them from me because you wanted me to find out and punish you. Now's your chance to come clean about one of them."

"I shoplifted from a store." She blurted out her teenage indiscretion quickly, the better to forestall discussions of any more recent transgressions.

"Is that recent?" he queried.

"No. I stole some makeup from the MAC counter at the Bay when I was fifteen."

"Was it only once?"

Once a week. More often if she could get a ride to the mall. But she wasn't going to confess the extent of her larcenous past to her lover. She just nodded a silent affirmation of his query.

"And more recently?"

"Do you remember the PowerPoint that Debbie messed up on at work and I said she lost out on a promotion?"

He nodded, then he grinned in disbelief. "Don't tell me... Jocelyn, did you fuck with a co-worker's presentation?"

"I did." She didn't feel bad about it either. Debbie was a bitch.

"Were you hoping to get the promotion yourself?" Sam didn't work with Jocelyn, but he had heard enough stories about her workmates and their antics at the office that he was as invested in her career as she was.

Jocelyn's dark curls rustled as she shook her head. "No. There's no way. I'm nowhere near qualified enough for that."

"Then why---?" Sams brow furrowed in puzzlement.

"I just didn't want her to get it. She's such a hag."

She loved it when she could surprise a laugh out of him. "You really are a piece of work Jocelyn." He kissed her thoroughly, his warm lips lingering against hers. "But I'm heading home soon. Do you want to hop into the bath before I go?" She loved it when he washed her back and shampooed her hair as part of their aftercare. But tonight, all this talk of Santa had her revved up again. She had a rendezvous in her bed with a dirty movie and her favourite non-kitchen appliance.

"I think I'm going to stay up a bit," she said. "I'm not very tired." She gave him a saucy grin. "Unless you want to punish me for being so naughty..."

He was already reaching for his clothes to get ready to go home. He paused in dressing to give her a smoldering look.

"I'm going to leave that for Santa..."

****

The package arrived on December 22nd. Jocelyn hadn't seen much of Sam in the weeks leading up to Christmas, but she hadn't expected to. His wife and kids demanded more of his time around the holidays.

Inside the package was a scandalous red teddy trimmed with white fur. There were thigh high white lace stockings and red heels to match. The accompanying note read: "December 24th. The safe word is Candy Cane."

Thankfully, Christmas Eve was on a Sunday, so Jocelyn didn't have to work. She spent the day cleaning her apartment and preparing for her nocturnal visitor. She built a cheerful fire up in the fireplace. If Santa was real, he would be pissed to find a fire blocking his route to her. Sam was at his most sexually creative when she gave him a reason to pretend to be angry with her. He was never actually angry – losing control emotionally was very dangerous in a BDSM relationship like theirs.

Santa traditionally snacked on milk and cookies. However, Sam wasn't a fan of sweets and Jocelyn was reasonably sure that any milk she put out would be warm and gross by the time they got around to taking a refreshment break. She set out some good red wine and a tray of nuts and dried fruits. She took care to buy shelled nuts. Nutcrackers freaked her out.

She ensured there was fresh bedding on the bed in the playroom, as well as laying all Sam's preferred toys within arms' reach. She showered and put on makeup and pulled her hair back into a bun. Sam liked to take her hair down as part of their prelude to play. She dressed carefully in the outfit he had bought her. She added some long dangling earrings that lightly brushed the curves of her bare shoulders. Finally, Jocelyn wound a jingly bell on a red ribbon around her finger. If she was unable to say her safe word and her hands were bound, the jingling of the bell would alert Sam that it was time to stop.

Jocelyn knew that some people in relationships like hers would await the arrival of their dominant partner on submissively bended knees. Sam's arrival time was never guaranteed, so spending hours on her knees only guaranteed leg cramps and a delay in starting play. Instead of kneeling, she had a low footstool she could sit on and wait for his arrival. She kept her cell phone nearby. If he couldn't come over, he would send a text message containing just a semicolon.

She positioned the footstool by the Christmas tree. All the lights in the room were dimmed – she was illuminated by the cheery glow from the fire and the incandescent light bulbs trimming her tree.

She leaned against the armchair by the footstool. The fire was keeping the room warm, and she was a bit tired from preparing. Playtime would go better if she was well rested. Surely it wouldn't hurt to close her eyes for just a minute…

"HO HO HO. What have we here?"

The raspy laugh startled Jocelyn awake. She let out a surprised bleat, her thickly lashed eyes flying open to see a figure looming over her.

Sam had really outdone himself with his costume. Every inch of him was perfectly Santa from the white pom pom at the end of the red hat down to the thick buckles that crossed over the arches of his big black boots.

His white bushy eyebrows drew down into a furrow while he studied her in turn. "So, this is how she turned out… little Joy Wiseman…"

Jocelyn didn't remember ever telling Sam her childhood family nickname. Her mother must have at some point. It had the effect of making her feel much younger and more unsure… and horny as hell.

"Tell me… Joy…" He drew her name out to what would be comical lengths if it wasn't for the heat in his gaze that was quickly being matched by heat suffusing other parts of Jocelyn's lingerie-clad body. "Have you been… naughty?" His voice dropped into Sam's lower register on the last word, bringing an answering shudder from Jocelyn.

"Yes..." She stared up at him gravely, her lower lip trembling.

The flat of his hand landed on her bare thigh, hard and heavy, leaving a stinging red mark.

"Yes... what?" he demanded.

"Yes... Santa..."

"Good girl..." His fingers stroked over the red marks, soothing the burn. She sighed. The white gloves he was wearing were so buttery soft. "Stand up," he ordered, stepping back. "Let me see how slutty you turned out. I should've known you were going to end up this way when you shoplifted that dildo in university..."

She knew she hadn't told Sam about that. He was probably just improvising, going off her story about having shoplifted in high school and knowing about her massive collection of sex toys she'd amassed long before she met Sam. But it was uncomfortably close to the truth – she had shoplifted a vibrator in university.

Santa sighed and snapped his fingers at her. "I'm not going to ask you twice, girl."

That was more like Sam. Not the finger snapping – that was a new quirk. But he was used to being obeyed on the first command. He didn't like to repeat himself.

Jocelyn rose to her feet and turned around slowly, giving him a full view of her body. Her curves were barely concealed by the lace and satin of the scandalous teddy.

He watched her in silence, then he jerked his head in a sideways gesture.

"Go stand by the tree," he ordered.

Jocelyn wondered if they were going to get freaky under the

tree. The only presents she had under the tree were for Sam and she was hoping he'd use them on her.

"Who are those presents for?"

"You..."

"You bought me presents? Nobody ever gets presents for Santa... Well, bring them to me..."

She brought him the first one and he quickly unwrapped it. The ball gag was seasonally themed with the rubber ball being striped in a candy cane pattern.

"I think we'll get some use out of that later..." he grinned.

"Do you want me to get you another present?" she asked.

"No." He snapped his fingers again. "Back to the tree."

She didn't think she liked this finger snapping thing. She'd have to find a way to mention it in aftercare.

"I think I need you moving less...." He came up to her. "Put your hands up above your head," he ordered. He reached behind her and unwound a length of silver and blue garland and used it to bind her wrists together and then to a branch above her. She was worried that the garland was too flimsy but when she carefully tried to pull her wrists apart, she found it held her effectively. Her next worry was the tree, but it seemed to be holding her sturdily. It would be a real mood killer if they had to stop play to rescue a fallen Christmas tree.

"Now I'm going to open my presents and you're going to stand there like a good girl. Can you do that, Joy? Or is Santa going to have to tape your mouth shut like the music teacher did?"

She knew she'd never told Sam that story. And neither had her mother because Joy had never told her. Maybe Tina had. She wouldn't put it past her, the bitch.

Santa opened the new paddles, restraints and nipple clamps and set them all aside. "These are all fun toys..." he said.

"But lucky for us, I brought my own..." He swung his sack up onto the footstool and began laying out items on the coffee table.

From the angle she was at, she couldn't get a clear view of the coffee table. It was delicious agony to hear the rustles and clinks of the gear he was laying out and try to guess what toys he'd brought. She hoped there were new things in there – this new roleplay of theirs had her feeling a bit more adventurous.

He finished laying out his tools and turned back to her. He stood with his hands on his hips and studied her.

"That is quite the outfit... it just needs one little touch..." He moved closer. One of his hands was clenched shut as though he was concealing something. She held her breath, wondering what it would be. Nipple clamps? Blindfold?

His free hand stroked the arch of her neck. She whimpered at the gentle kiss of the leather gloves. Both hands moved and she felt something slipping around her neck.

No.

Hell no.

Sam knew she didn't like things around her neck. Breath play was a hard no from her. She debated using her safe word and decided to wait a moment to see where he was going with it.

"There." He moved away so she had an unobstructed view of herself in the hall mirror. He had added a large red satin bow tied neatly around her neck. "Now you're all wrapped up for Christmas..."

She relaxed. It was just a bit of costuming. She had to admit it added a certain rakish festivity to her sexy outfit.

"And now we tighten the bow..." He stepped in front of her, his hands reaching for the bow again.

It was time to remind him that she didn't do breath play.

"Candy cane..." She hated to safe word so early, but she

didn't want to succumb to the kind of screaming panic attack that would derail the rest of their night.

"Oh, no thank you…" He chuckled, patting his round stomach playfully. "Trying to watch my weight…"

She thought he was just playing the Santa role to the hilt and that he'd gotten her message. Then his hands reached for the bow again.

"Candy cane." She said it louder, more definitely. It was time to stop this and move to something else.

"I said no." His voice was sharp. His hands seized the edges of her bow and started to pull it more snugly. The satin pressed against her skin. Even though her airway wasn't yet compressed, her chest started heaving as she began to hyperventilate in anticipation.

"Candy cane!" She'd never had to raise her voice in scene. But then again, Sam had never ignored her safe word.

It made him pull his hands away from the ribbon.

"I am getting tired of your whining." He reached down and his hand settled on the ball gag. "I guess it's time for this. Open up, Joy."

The ball gag was familiar territory and she accepted it willingly.

"Better." He stepped back again, and she caught a view of herself in the mirror. Her face was blotchy and her eyes a bit watery, but overall, she still looked sexy as hell, even more so with the addition of the ball gag. Her pounding heart slowed into anticipatory throbs of their evening getting back on track and into familiar territory.

"Now…" He chuckled. "You've been a very bad girl. I've been watching you."

He knew how to push her buttons. She loved the idea of

being watched from afar, stalked by a sexual predator. It was a game they sometimes played.

"Ever since you were a wee girl, you've been a holy terror, haven't you, Joy?"

She wished he'd call her "Jocelyn". It was unsettling to have him continually using the name she'd gone by in her previous life before she'd grown up and moved away from her small hometown. But now that she was gagged, she couldn't make any requests. She could only flutter her eyelashes at him and jingle her bell if things got too intense.

"There are so many things we should address tonight.... I hope you're comfortable Joy. Are you?" He didn't look to her to see if she was going to answer. "It doesn't matter. You've never taken anyone else's comfort into account other than your own, have you? Not even once."

He surveyed the collection of toys on the coffee table. "Now where do we start... do we do it chronologically or in the order of severity...." He tapped his chin thoughtfully.

Jocelyn was uneasy at the direction this was taking. She decided to stop the scene. Sam would untie her; they could discuss why she was upset, and they could maybe come up with another scenario that wasn't quite so disturbing.

She twitched the ring finger of her left hand, making the bell jingle.

He didn't move and didn't look at her.

She jingled again, a bit harder.

"Stop jingling," he said, "I'm thinking."

She jingled again.

"If you jingle that damned bell again, I'm going to cut your fucking finger off," he growled.

The threat shocked her into stillness. They never played

with violent threats in the eighteen months they'd been experimenting with BDSM. The most he'd ever threaten her with was a spanking if she didn't stop being a brat. Sometimes she obeyed but most times she'd keep pushing the limits until she ended up facedown over his knee with his hand landing firmly on her bare bottom. That was sexy fun.

Being threatened with dismemberment was not.

"Well, if we start with the worst thing first, the games will be over now."

She would be okay with that – even if it hurt more than she wanted, at least this uncomfortable scene would be over, and they could move on to aftercare where he would cuddle her, and she could tell him she never wanted to "Santa scene" again. It was safe to say she was cured of this particular kink.

"I don't want the games to be over yet. I still have a few minutes before I must go punish some other bad girls and boys." There was movement and then he approached her.

"First there was the time you stole that makeup…"

He bent low over her thigh, dragging something soft in a slow pattern. He moved to her other thigh and repeated the process.

"There." He stood back so she could see herself in the mirror. "I wrote the words backwards so even a dumb bunny like you could understand them."

One thigh had the word "thief" written on it in lipstick. The other thigh displayed the word "whore".

"Just so you don't forget who you are."

Sam had written words on her body before during scenes – being "slut shamed" was one of her kinks. It was familiar territory. Jocelyn tried to assure herself that they were on their way back to their usual normal abnormality.

Sam selected another item from his assortment and turned back to her.

"It's time you paid for putting Tina out in the snow..." His fingertips gently pulled the elastic leg hole away from the crux of where her leg met her torso. They slipped inside her teddy. She shivered from the coolness of whatever he held in his hand. Ice. He was putting ice into her teddy. It was a fitting punishment for having put Tina out in the snow in just her underwear. Poetic justice.

Jocelyn shuddered as the chunk found its ultimate destination. The cold against her tender intimate flesh was a thrilling contrast. It quickly passed the line from pleasurable to excruciating. It felt like she was blistering from the cold. Her body thrashed in reaction to the invasion of the piercing sensations emanating from her core. Even with her shudders and struggles, she folded her finger tightly to prevent any errant tinkling. She was in agony from the rampant bitter freezing.

He stood back so she could witness the wisps of fog drifting from her crotch.

"It's dry ice," he told her. "We need to dry you up," he joked.

Her lips parted wider, and she tried to scream through the gag. A strangled "Ugh ugh ugh" was the best she could manage. She forced her legs apart and her hips bucked, trying to expel the dry ice from her teddy.

His gloved fingers seized her chin. He leaned in closer to stare into her eyes.

"Now stop that," he ordered, "You wanted Santa to punish you. Well, here I am." His blue eyes narrowed with his icy glare.

Blue eyes.

Sam's eyes were hazel. He had very sensitive eyes. He couldn't ever wear contacts.

This wasn't Sam.

With that realization, Jocelyn sagged back against the tree. The bristly branches scratched and poked at her skin. She was alone with some maniac dressed as Santa who was intent upon hurting her.

She had to get out of here. She began struggling hard against the garland that was holding her to the tree. It was just garland. Surely, she could break free of it. The harder she flailed, the tighter her bonds became.

"You're not getting out of those," he declared. "If it's good enough to keep eight tiny reindeer secured to the sleigh, it's more than good enough to hold one deceitful little bitch in place."

She tried to scream through the gag again, pitching her voice higher and shriller. She screamed herself hoarse while he watched in amusement, his arms folded casually across his chest.

"Go on," he encouraged playfully. "Get it out of your system. Nobody's going to come. Nobody cares. Sam's home with his wife and kids. Your neighbours are all visiting their families. Nobody cares about a stupid slut like you."

She unclenched her fist and started waving her finger frantically, sending the bell pealing. It was her last hope.

His jovial smile quickly changed to a thunderous scowl. "I said no jingling!" He grabbed something from the table and charged at her. His hand seized her wrist, holding it tightly.

His other hand darted up. It felt like he smacked her ring finger. There was a dull thudding sensation like a flogger against bare skin and then a rush of warmth that flooded her hand and arm. She thought that maybe he hadn't carried through on his threat about cutting her finger off.

Until she saw her left ring finger bouncing across the room, the ribbon unspooling behind it, mixing with the streamers that were flowing from the severed blood vessels.

Santa watched the finger on its erratic path across the

room. The bell broke free of the ribbon and spiralled under the couch, jingling all the way. "Fitting that it's your ring finger," he mused. "Since nobody's ever going to put a ring on it, are they, Joy?"

The warmth on her hand and arm was her blood. The world tilted and went grey.

A sharp pain on her inner thigh brought her back. His fingers poised, ready to pinch again if it looked like she was about to faint.

"Now we can't have you checking out before the finale," he admonished. "It wouldn't be nice. And I've come all this way at your request." He grinned. "I don't often get the chance to punish naughty girls like this, so thank you Joy. But sadly, our time here tonight is at an end. I do have to make some deliveries to the good girls and boys. So, tell me, Joy… do you remember Franklin?"

Franklin Hodges. Her grade nine boyfriend. She hadn't thought of him in years. She'd pushed the memories firmly out of her mind.

"I know you like to tell yourself it wasn't your fault… But it's confession time, Joy. It really is, isn't it? Weren't you the one who convinced him that sex would be so much hotter if he let you tie his hoodie to the door? You're just lucky nobody saw you leave after the…. What did you tell yourself? After the accident? It wasn't, was it, Joy? You watched it happen, you didn't go for help, and you ran before anyone found you. His poor parents still believe he killed himself…"

His hands seized the ends of the bow around her neck. He leaned in closer as he began to tighten them.

"When you get to hell, say hello to Franklin…"

****

After midnight. He would have gotten here sooner but the kids wanted "just one more story" and then his wife wanted help setting up the kids' toys. Both the kids and wife had gotten a kick out of the Santa costume. He'd rented it for some sexy time with his mistress, but he'd seen no reason why he couldn't do double duty and score dad and husband points with his family. Until they ended up eating up most of his evening.

Sam cursed under his breath as he fought to get the unfamiliar bulk of the padded Santa suit out of his Honda. He reached in the backseat for the bag of toys. He'd had a lot of fun ordering them from discrete online boutiques and then wrapping them in the safety of his office, imagining the many ways he was going to use them on Jocelyn, his sweet and sassy little submissive.

Blue and red lights washed over the front of her apartment building in strobing patterns. Somebody's Christmas was off to a rough start.

The area was cordoned off with yellow and black tape. He'd only seen that in crime shows. He was so fascinated by it that he almost crossed the line, but he was stopped by a uniformed police officer.

"Do you live here?" the officer demanded.

"Yes," Sam lied. His preoccupation with the police markers was being replaced by concern for Jocelyn. He needed to get in to see her, to ensure she was all right.

"Can I see proof?" The officer held out his hand.

"Proof?" Sam repeated the word, feeling thick.

"Driver's license, utility bill, something with your address on it," the officer rhymed off tiredly.

Sam tried for levity. "Santa doesn't carry identification."

"Then Santa can go cool his happy ass off with the others and wait until we can sort it out." The officer pointed to a crowd of people standing off to the side. Sam recognized one or two of them as people who lived in the building. He'd seen them coming and going on the nights he'd been having trysts with Jocelyn in her sixth-floor apartment.

He joined the crowd, trying to eavesdrop, secure in his anonymity in his Santa costume.

"What's going on?"

"I heard someone got killed."

"Who?"
"Girl on the sixth floor."
"Not the Martinez girl."

"No not the teenager. That one who lived by herself. End of the hall."

Sam's stomach churned. He knew exactly who they were talking about. Jocelyn was the only girl who lived by herself on that floor. The other tenants were either families or retired couples. He slunk back into the shadows. The last thing he needed to be doing was be discovered dressed as Santa with a bag full of sex toys outside the apartment of a murdered girl he'd been having an affair with. His wife Monica was forgiving of many things, but this would be the deal breaker. He turned away and for a second, he thought he was seeing himself reflected in a shop window. Another Santa stood there. Sam regarded him in silence for a moment, then gave him a brusque nod as he passed by on the way back to his sleigh, which was a late model navy blue Honda.

The other Santa returned the nod and then spoke softly.

"And to all a good night…"

CHRISTMAS DAY

Christmas Day. The big event. The extravaganza we've been gearing up for over the past weeks. It's the light in the darkness, the song that breaks the silence…and for many people not the most wonderful time of the year. Suicides increase over Christmas. There is an uptick in people filing for divorce come the New Year. I've worked in health care my entire career and while the death rate actually declines on Christmas Day, a lot of our palliative patients glide away either in the days before or immediately after.

Family togetherness is almost mandated at this time of the year. The big meals, the exchanging of gifts, the goodwill towards all and blessings for everyone. What if you don't have a family? What if you have a family but you don't like them? It's an aberration to admit to either during this festive season, so we pretend. We pretend to like our families. We pretend to like the weird side dishes that our weird relatives brought (marshmallows, lime Jell-O and carrots? Okay….), and we pretend to like our presents. We pretend to a level of seasonal happiness akin to the most excited game show contestant and maintain it in the face of any and all domestic disasters.

Nobody wants to ruin Christmas. Well, almost nobody…

AIR PODS AND EAR WORMS

The only thing more extreme than a child's excitement on Christmas morning is the child's disappointment when they don't get what they want...

As soon as Maddy opened the box she started sobbing. She threw it down and ran from the living room, the untied belt of her robe flapping behind her.

"What is going on?" Jessica stared after their daughter. Thirteen-year-olds were prone to dramatics, but this was extreme even for Maddy. It had been a lovely Christmas morning until just now.

Jessica fished for the discarded box amidst the drifts of wrapping paper. She immediately gleaned the reason for the outburst. "Knock offs? Really, Steven?"

Steve knew he was in the doghouse. Jessica never used his full name. "I wasn't going to spend three hundred dollars for ear buds," he protested. "She'd lose one. You know she would. Probably before Christmas Day was over."

Jessica ignored his rationale and waved the offending box at him. "It was the only thing she wanted for Christmas. That and an Apple Music gift card so she could download the latest 5 Seconds of Summer album. I got her the gift card. And the new sweater. And those boots. You had one job Steven. One."

"Three hundred dollars," he bleated.

"And now she's crying," Jessica pointed out. "Is three hundred dollars worth your daughter's happiness?"

He hated it when Jessica resorted to emotional blackmail. There was only way to get back into her good graces. He was going to have to make the ultimate sacrifice.

Steve was going to have to go out on Boxing Day.

Steve was up and out the door before dawn the next day. He had the Boxing Day sales flyers piled into the passenger seat of the family minivan and one mission in mind – buy Air Pods for his daughter. At least he wasn't going to have to pay the full three hundred, but it was small consolation. The day after Christmas was for sleeping late, eating leftover Christmas food, and playing with new toys. Steve had a drone he was eager to try out, but instead here he was prowling the parking lot at the mall like a creep, trying to remember which of the doors was closest to the Apple store.

He finally found a parking spot. It was a far hike away from the mall doors. It served him right -waiting until six-thirty to leave the house instead of being out the door at four like the rest of the deal-crazed shoppers.

Snow crunched under his feet as he trudged his way to the mall doors. They admitted him with an indifferent 'whoosh'. He could see the line for the Apple store already stretched halfway down the concourse – weaving in and out of the lines for Justice, Hot Topic and LUSH – the four pillars of any tween's life. His shoulders settled into a resigned slump, and he joined the shuffling processional toward the monolithic fruit.

Steve didn't know how long he waited in the line. It seemed to move forward by bare inches. An ache settled into his lower back, and he shifted his weight from one foot to the other, hoping to forestall the ache turning into spasms. He'd had a bout of sciatica once and he was in no hurry to repeat the experience.

"Some line, hey?"

At first Steve didn't register that the man behind him was speaking to him, until the back of a hand gently prodded him. "Some line, yeah?" The man repeated his earlier query with a slightly different inflection.

"Yeah." Steve nodded and kept his eyes trained to the front. The Apple store had a big glass door and a staff member keeping watch at it, ensuring that only a prescribed number of patrons were in the store at any given time. Steve started playing a game with himself, trying to guess how many more times the door would open and close before it was his turn.

"I gotta return these." A small white box danced at the periphery of Steves view. "I got my kid Air Pods. He didn't want'em. Wanted some of those, what d'ya call'em… Beats?" The man chuckled. "Either way it's a fruit or a vegetable, right?"

"Sure." Steve bobbed his head quickly. He didn't want to encourage the man behind him. He just wanted to get Maddy her Air Pods and get home so he could play with his drone.

"This line is taking forever though," the man commented. "Hey, what're you in for?"

Steve almost said, "murder" and followed it up with a threatening glare, but that really wasn't his style. "Bought my kid knock offs. She had a fit. So now I'm buying her the real ones."

"Hey, you wanna buy mine?" the man offered. He read the hesitancy in Steve's body language. "Look, this line is gonna go on for hours. I want to just get my kid the Beats, go home, be father of the year and then have a nice scotch and watch It's a Wonderful Life."

That did sound good to Steve.

"Here's what I'm thinking," the guy continued. "The ones my boy wants are about a hundred and fifty. The ones your girl wants are on sale for two seventy-five. You give me two. I'll give you these, you save seventy-five, I make fifty and we're both home before lunch. Sound good?" The man showed him the little white box he was carrying. Steve looked it over. They were the ones Maddy wanted. The box was in pristine condition.

"Did he try them on?" Steve didn't like the thought of something that had been in some other kid's ear being shoved into his daughter's ear.

"Nope." The other man sighed. "He looked at them, threw them at me and ran to his bedroom to have a tantrum."

Steve felt a kinship to this other beleaguered father who was just trying to do right by his ungrateful kid. Even though something about the math didn't seem right, Steve found himself agreeing to the trade.

The two men slipped out of the line and to the food court nearby. Steve stopped at a bank machine to withdraw the money. The exchange was made and in no time at all Steve was on his way home.

Maddy was overjoyed with the new ear buds. She smothered her dad in hugs and kisses before racing off to try them out.

Steve spent a pleasant afternoon playing with his drone and then having a nap. Apart from his morning excursion, it was shaping up to be a very good Boxing Day.

Leftover turkey was one of his favourite dinners and he was happy to see the table laden with the remnants of yesterday's feast like a visit from the gastronomic Ghost of Christmas Past. He was less happy to see Maddy arrive at the table with her ear buds still in place.

She sat down at her spot at the table and turned her gaze down to stare at the shiny white surface of her plate. She seemed to be lost in thought – or at least in the music being pumped into her ears.

"Maddy."

She ignored Steve. She stared down at her plate, her lips moving as she mouthed the lyrics to the song.

"Maddy." He raised his voice. She didn't look up.

"Madison!" Full names were usually an indication of trouble. She didn't even flinch. Steve glared at Jessica, giving her one chance to intervene before he escalated.

"Maddy, honey…" Jessica reached over to touch Maddy's hand. Their daughter jerked and her head came up. She seemed to just realize that she was in the dining room. It was almost as though she'd been sleepwalking, and Jessica had roused her.

"Is it dinner time?" Maddy blinked owlishly at her parents.

"It is." Jessica gestured to the ear buds. "Please take those out so we can have some peace."

"Can I just finish this song? It's totally supreme – I've been listening to it over and over again. I can't get it out of my head. It's one of those snake things… you know like when you hear the song over and over."

"Ear worm, honey," Steve corrected her, "But yes, it's an ear worm." He shook his head at Maddy. "And you can listen after supper, Mads. Let's give the 5 Seconds of Summer boys a rest, okay?"

She reluctantly surrendered the ear buds to eat dinner with her family. She raced through the clean up chores after supper and then back to her room for more listening time.

"She really likes those ear buds." Jessica handed Steve a glass of wine. "Did you have trouble getting them? I know they were a hot ticket item."

"No, it was easy." He wasn't about to tell her that he'd bought them from a random stranger in a clandestine food court tech deal. Jessica was funny about things like that.

"And you're going to take the knock offs back to… wherever you got them from?"

"Uh huh." Steve took a sip of his wine. It was so good he took another sip and then another.

"Once you've finished your wine, maybe we should go upstairs, and you can unwrap one more Christmas present…" Jessica wiggled her eyebrows suggestively.

Steve didn't need a second invitation. Within minutes, the wine was finished, and he was escorting a giggling Jessica to their bedroom.

Jessica stretched out on the bed, and he set about getting her out of her pyjamas. He kissed and caressed every inch of her skin.

As he was kissing his way along the curve of her neck, he became aware that she was humming softly. He paused.

"Are you… humming?"

She giggled. "It's that song," she admitted. "Maddy let me listen to it. It really is infectious."

He tried to keep going, but his interest started to flag in the face of the breathy tune being murmured by his partner. "Jess. Please."

She giggled again. "Sorry." She was silent while he returned to the task of disrobing her. He caressed one of her more sensitive spots and she moaned in response. The moan soon slid into a soft upward lilt that became that damned song.

"Jess…" he growled. It was becoming more difficult to sustain the momentum of the seduction.

"Sorry Steve…" she apologized again.

He turned his attention to parts of her further away from the delicate bridge of her neck. Hopefully he wouldn't be able to hear the humming down at her legs. He began feathering slow touches along her inner thighs, each stroke moving higher and higher.

Her legs seemed to vibrate with the hum emanating from her. That damn song.

He sat up abruptly.

"Steve? Where are you going?"

"I just need a drink of water." Maybe if he left her alone for a few minutes she'd lay off the song.

In the bathroom across the hall from their bedroom, he filled the glass and drank it dry twice. He splashed a bit of water on his face. He swished some mouthwash around and spit into the sink.

There was a glow coming out from under Maddy's door. He glanced at his watch. It was after midnight. School wasn't back in yet, but it was still too late for her to be up.

He tapped lightly on her door. "Maddy?" There was no answer. "Mads?" Still no reply. He wondered if she'd fallen asleep with her light on. It had been known to happen. He eased the door open, fingers stretching out to find the light switch and save their electric bill.

Maddy was on her bed, staring up at the ceiling and humming. That damn song.

"Maddy!" His voice was a sharp crack that made her sit up with a start.

She pulled one of her ear buds out, wincing. "Sorry Dad." She smiled sheepishly. "I guess I was really into the song."

"It's late," he pointed out. "Go to sleep. You can listen more tomorrow."

"Yes, Dad." She put her phone beside her bed.

"Here." He held his hand out. "Let me take it down and put it on the charger for you." He wasn't a rookie. He knew if he didn't take it away, she'd be back on it the moment the door closed behind him.

Her cheeks pinked as she realized he was onto her. She meekly handed over her phone and the treasured ear buds.

He took her phone and the buds downstairs to charge overnight. By the time he had plugged them in, turned off the lights that had been left on, checked the front door, and made his way back to the bedroom, Jessica was asleep.

The moment lost, Steve laid down beside his wife and drifted off to dream of a world where all the music came on cassette tapes, and nobody had ever heard of 5 Seconds of Summer.

• •

"Does Maddy seem different to you?" Steve slid the bottle of champagne into the fridge as he posed the question.

"Hmm?" There was an upwards lilt at the end of Jessica's vocalization – almost as though she were about to start humming. She caught the warning wrinkle of his nose and coughed. "Um. Not really. Why?"

Steve shrugged. It wasn't anything he could put his finger on. His daughter had seemed more distant and withdrawn in the days since Boxing Day. He'd wondered if there was some kind of female thing going on with her, but he had no idea how to ask that. "She just seems… different. Like today when Katy called and invited her over. She said no. Since when has Maddy ever passed on the chance to hang out with Katy?"

"Maybe she has something better to do." Jessica pulled out the block of cheese and started cutting slices to add to the charcuterie board.

"Like listen to that stupid song over and over again?" Steve started laying crackers out on the wooden tray.

"It's not stupid." Jessicas voice was sharp, and it stung. Steve recoiled. She noticed and gave him a wobbly smile. "Sorry. I didn't mean to snap at you. Just not sleeping well. Too much holiday goodness. I'm glad tomorrow's New Year's Day. We can start trying to get back to some semblance of normalcy."

"Thank goodness." Steve surveyed their handiwork. "The annual Evans family cheese and cracker fest is ready to start."

Ever since Maddy had been small and the costs of going out on New Year's Eve proved to be prohibitive to a young couple, the family had the tradition of ringing in the New Year in front of the TV with trays of snacks.

"Did you pick up the noisemakers?" Jessica asked.

"They're already in the family room," Steve said.

Steve had been afraid he was going to have to chase Maddy down from her room to spend time with the family, but she was already perched on the ottoman, alternating her attention between the screen of the TV and the screen of the phone she held in her hand.

He tried to figure out a greeting that wouldn't upset her. He didn't want to have to deal with pre-teen tantrums tonight. Steve wanted to start the New Year off right. He settled for, "I'm glad you're here."

"5 Seconds of Summer is performing tonight." Her reply was delivered with the air of "you should have known that". In the interests of preserving familial peace, he chose not to rise to the implied condescension.

Jessica joined him on the couch, passing out drinks and napkins. For the next couple of hours, it felt like every other New Year's Eve – there was a lot of food, a lot of laughter and a lot of fun. They made fun of the lamer musical acts and talked during the commercials. When a band from their youth performed, Jessica and Steve bored their daughter with tales of their teen years.

Maddy's band took the stage at eleven-thirty. Jessica and Maddy stopped talking mid-sentence. They both turned to watch the boy band dancing and singing. They sang one song and then Steve heard the all too familiar and much-loathed opening bars of that song.

"I can't. I'm out." He stood up. It was time to start pouring the traditional midnight toasts anyhow. "Call me back if they spontaneously combust or something else interesting happens."

In the kitchen he poured three drinks – champagne for the adults, sparkling grape juice for the child. He arranged a few pieces of fruit on a tray with a tub of chocolate dip in the centre and surrounded by chocolate truffles and cookies. The midnight chocolate feast was another of their traditions. Leaving the drinks on the counter for the moment, he carried the tray into the living room.

Nobody was in the living room. He looked at the deserted sofa and ottoman. Maybe they'd gone upstairs to use the facilities before the big countdown started. He settled on the couch to wait.

They hadn't reappeared by the time the large digital timer on the screen had started to wind down the last few seconds of the old year.

Steve sighed. "I guess it's just me..." He counted off under his breath as the crowd in New York sang and cheered their way into the New Year. "Happy New Year." He raised his glass and drained it. "Happy New Year to me." He set the empty glass on the coffee table and left the remnants of their celebration. They could wait for morning. He was going to bed.

Maddy's bedroom light was on. He debated going in and getting her to hang up her ear buds for the night. He decided it wasn't the war he wanted to fight tonight.

Jessica was lying crosswise on their bed. Her head was on her pillow, but her feet were over on his side.

"Jess... Hey, come on bed hog..." He nudged her feet. "Move on over, Chiquita..."

Jessica didn't move. Her head was in shadows. The only light in the room was coming from the table lamp on his side of the bed. He reached to flip on the overhead light.

Jessica's brown eyes were wide, staring up at the ceiling, staring into nothing. Her lips were parted – no wrenched – wrenched open. A long slick trail of saliva traced from the corner of her mouth down along her jawline to puddle in the deep shadows behind her ear.

"Jessica?" His voice rose desperately into a near screech. "Jess?" He shook her roughly. His wife did not move. He lurched closer and saw her chest rise slightly and then fall, her breath leaving her chest in a slow wheezing rattle. He saw one of Maddy's ear buds half-hidden by a fold of blanket. His fingers closed around it, and he shoved it into his pocket.

Steve had to get help. His cell phone was downstairs, sitting in the charger beside Jessica's. He soundly cursed their decision to get rid of their landline. The empty spot where their bedroom phone had once sat mocked him.

He knew where there was a cell phone. It seemed he was going to have to fight this war after all. His wife's life was worth a teenage tantrum.

"Maddy!" Her door thundered against the wall under the force of his fist. She was lying on her bed, air pods snugged into her ears. "Maddy your mom is sick. Give me your phone."

She didn't respond. Her eyes were closed. She was humming that infernal song.

"Maddy!" He'd had enough of this nonsense. Two strides brought him beside her bed. He grabbed the pod in her ear and yanked. He'd pull the damn thing out and then he'd stomp it to pieces.

The pod put up unexpected resistance. He pulled harder, really heaving at it, pinching the pod tightly between his fingers.

The pod felt pliable, sticky, and unnaturally warm in his grasp. The thick pink strand that stretched from the pod into her ear writhed as he exposed it to the light. He jerked it harder, trying to dislodge it. Maddy's eyes flew open, and she screamed – a long bloodcurdling screech that almost brought him to his knees. He felt his legs shake, his innards feeling liquid and crampy in response to his daughter's tortured wails. He felt something thick and dark rising in his gorge in response to the pink squirming thing sticking out of his daughter's ear.

Steve's trembling fingers released the pod. It slithered back into her ear, seating itself deep into the canal. Maddy stopped screaming and returned to humming.

The air pods. He'd done this. Brought this foul thing into their house that had stolen his wife and daughter. They were lost to him forever and it was his fault. His. There was only one thing Steve could do.

The other air pod was still in his pocket. Steve grabbed the air pod and put it in his ear.

I'LL BE HOME FOR CHRISTMAS

… you can plan on me …

"What kind of moron schedules a free climb for a week before Christmas?" Shyla scowled, hoping her displeasure was being adequately broadcast over the tenuous connection.

"The same kind of moron who is unbearably in love with you." Ryan was unabashed by her evident scorn. "I'm leaving right after the climb, Shy," he promised. "I'll be home before you know it. I'll be home for Christmas." He sang the last sentence.

"Don't."

"I can't resist, Shy, you know me."

Shyla traced her thumb over his wavering image on the square screen. "Hurry home, Ry." Shy and Ry – high school sweethearts. The impossible cuteness of their rhyming names.

"Promise."

"Home for Christmas," she insisted.

"Home for Christmas," he repeated. He grinned. "Maybe I'll have something shiny and sparkly that wraps around your finger," he hinted. "Now let me talk to my useless brother."

Trevor was already there, his hand reaching for the phone. Shyla relinquished it. She couldn't stand to listen to the two of them carrying on with their juvenile jokes and quips that hid their deep affection. God, boys were stupid. Couldn't they ever just say they loved each other?

"Can I help you?" Trevor's girlfriend Emma joined Shyla in the kitchen.

Shyla nodded and the two of them worked together to assemble a tray of assorted snacks for the viewing party gathered in the living room.

"Got your Christmas shopping done?" Emma was trying to distract Shyla from her trepidation over Ryan's climb.

Shyla appreciated the effort. "Mostly, yeah. How about you?"

Emma nodded. "Yeah."

"Hey Shy! Ryan wants to mack on you some more!" Trevor came into the kitchen to hand the phone to Shyla. Emma passed him one of the trays.

"Here. Let's make ourselves useful and let the two lovebirds have their moment." Emma and Trevor bickered as they left the kitchen.

"I love you," Shyla said.

"I love you," Ryan answered. "Less than a week. I'll be home."

"I know." She nodded. She wouldn't cry. She wouldn't. He would be home. He always came home.

"Now let me go appease the fans and sponsors. You going to watch?"

"No." She never watched his free climbs. She just couldn't.

"Good." It made him less nervous to know she wasn't watching him. "Love you."

He ended the call before she could respond. He always did. The last word had to be his. It was one of his many pre-climb rituals. She knew he was wearing the same underwear he always did, but that he had brand new socks on fresh out of the package. His breakfast that morning would have been an espresso from

Wholly Beans, one of his sponsors, and two granola bars from Good Times Grainery, another of his sponsors. Ryan called his sponsors his "Necessary Evils". He had to livestream so many of his free climbs a year to keep their financial support, but it was having that support that had allowed him to quit his job in the nine to five corporate world and live out his dreams of climbing every surface he could find.

Trevor and Emma were gathered in the living room with several of their friends. Shyla couldn't bear to go out there. They had Ryan up on the big flatscreen so they could watch his live stream.

Shyla settled on a chair in the doorway. She kept her back to the screen. Listening to his outrageously colourful commentary was the most she could do, and it had taken her months to get that far. She used to leave the apartment altogether when he was livestreaming one of his climbs. The timeless irony of an agoraphobic being in a relationship with a thrill-seeking heights junkie.

There was a sharp buzz and then Ryan's cheerful voice filled the room. "Hey there freaks, it's your boy Ryan about to climb the imposing Mount Possible, way out in Rickrack BC. As always, super shout out to Gnarly Climbing Supplies, Moose Foot Socks, and Cool Lid caps for my gear, Wholly Beans and Good Times Grainery for filling my belly and Foxy Rental Cars for my sweet ride here. Special shout outs to my bro Trev, his girl Emma, and my special girl Shyla. Can't wait to see you baby, but gotta make the fans happy first. So, freaks, let's get the technical deets out of the way. Mount Possible is a class four. I'm going up the south face, which is the gnarliest side. For climbing today I'm rocking my favourite hat from Cool Lids. It's got the best hands-free rigging to keep my phone high and dry. I have my new Moose Foot socks on in red and green stripes – very Christmassy. My belly is full of Wholly Beans' new campfire roasted espresso and a chocolate PB bar from Good Times Grainery. Gonna make a shout out here to Gnarly

Climbing's new line of pitons. If you buy them right now and use the code "ShysGuyRy", you'll get five percent off, free shipping and a cool free gift if you spend more than seventy-five smackeroos." Rustles and clinks telegraphed to Shyla that he was positioning himself for ascent. He wore a camera on his hat that would record the climb, immersing the viewer and making them feel like they were along with Ryan on the climb.

"So here we go. It's a chilly day up here in the mountain range and there's a low hanging cloud cover. Snow in the forecast, so I'd better get my move on." There were rustles.

"He's off the ground." Trevor knew Shyla's fears and he knew exactly how much information she needed to keep them at bay. "His form is good, Shy. No worries."

"No worries," she whispered. Her hands knotted anxiously in her lap. She had a plate with some cheese and crackers and veggies and dip on the counter, but she couldn't eat. Her mouth felt dry and pasty. She took a small sip of her water. It was difficult to even swallow that.

Everyone's breath caught in a collective gasp from the living room. Shyla couldn't look. Wouldn't look.

"Oops," Ryan chuckled, "That was not a handhold, freaks. Remember, test with your hand before you swing your weight over."

"He's all right, Shy," Trevor called out, "You know he likes to fake out the audience. Gets more clicks."

She knew. It didn't make it any easier from where she sat.

"Oh, hey, it's starting to snow. Maybe I should sing some Christmas carols." Ryan laughed. "Or maybe if you all donate to the Salvation Army Christmas fund, I won't. Your choice, freaks."

The rest of the climb continued with Ryan's trademark quips interspersed with shout outs to his sponsors and climbing advice. Ryan was one of the most followed free climbers on

YouTube and his livestreamed climbs were usually watched by thousands of fans worldwide.

"I'm up to the summit." He'd been at it for almost an hour. The sweet spot for climbs was just about the forty-five-to-fifty-minute mark. Any shorter and fans felt cheated. Any longer and they would get bored. The short attention span of the Internet generation. "One last handhold and then the flag goes up and I come down." There was a rustle, then Ryan's voice said in a tone that was conversationally apologetic, "Fuck." It was followed by an ominous cracking sound and then a series of dull thuds and hollow clatters punctuated by several grunts from Ryan.

Then nothing.

The silence in her living room was more ominous than the lack of noise from the television. It was so quiet Shyla swore she could hear the sound of snowflakes falling, dotting the rocky outcrops of Mount Possible, way up in northern BC where the dreadful quiet just kept spinning out into an eternity.

"What's going on?" Shyla started to turn, but Emma was there.

"Let's not look at the screen, okay Shyla?" Emma put her hands gently on Shyla's shoulders. She held Shyla gently but firmly, preventing her from turning to look at the television screen.

In the living room Trevor was on his phone. "What do you mean you can't get up there tonight… Fuck the snow, my brother's up there and he might be hurt… Listen here, fuckers, if you don't go get my brother there will be a lawsuit…" Trevor looked up from his cell phone. "They hung up."

Shyla pulled away from Emma's embrace and wandered into the living room, brushing past the friends who tried to touch her, to hug her, to turn her away from the large flatscreen television that dominated one wall of the room.

Ryan had fallen sideways. The camera showed a ground level view of rocks. The lens of the camera was being quickly obscured by falling snow. It wasn't covered enough yet that Shyla couldn't see the wide swatch of red that covered the face of one rock, glistening wetly in the rapidly diminishing light.

Shyla grabbed her phone and tried to start a video chat with Ryan. On screen they could hear the buzz of his phone.

"Hi, this is Ryan. If you're getting this message, I'm probably sleeping or climbing. Go to www.shysguyry.ca to find out which one it is. Ciao, freaks!"

Even though she knew it was futile, she tried. "It's Shy. Get up baby. You're coming home for Christmas. You promised." Her hand tightened around the phone. She screamed, "You promised!"

"Okay, Shyla, enough of that..." Emma took the phone gently away. "Do you have someone who can come sit with you?"

"I have Ryan." Shyla's lips felt numb and cold, like she'd just had the worlds biggest Novocain injection.

"Shyla..." Emma said gently, then looked helplessly at the other friends in the room.

"I've got her." Shyla's friend Grace came forward. "I can spend the night here."

"I have to... I have to go tell my dad..." Trevor seemed to be sleepwalking. Shyla knew how he felt.

"Yes." Emma wiped her eyes. "I'll drive, Trev."

"Shyla should come," Trevor insisted, "You shouldn't be alone."

"I'm not alone. Ryan will be here..."

"Oh Shyla..." Trevor's lip trembled.

"It's okay," Grace assured them, "I'll stay here tonight."

Trevor nodded. "I'm going to my dad's place. Maybe he can

talk those fuckers into going to get Ryan. He can't stay out there. It's snowing. He's going to be so cold."

Nobody pointed out that Ryan was far beyond feeling cold ever again.

The rest of the guests left one at a time, everyone hugging Shyla and promising they'd be in touch, and she should let them know if she needed anything. Shyla nodded and accepted hugs and promises and platitudes with a detached air. It wasn't real. It couldn't be real. There was no way.

After they'd left, Grace ordered pizza for the two of them and coaxed Shyla into eating half a slice. She wanted to turn the television off, to cancel the view, which was now just drifts of white.

Shyla wouldn't let her. It seemed like she was cutting off the last connection with Ryan. The camera batteries would only last so long and then it would just stop broadcasting. Maybe she'd be able to let go then.

It was after midnight before Grace could convince Shyla to go to bed. Shyla changed into her favourite nightie and lay on her back, staring up at the ceiling in her darkened bedroom. Ryan had pasted glow in the dark stars up there in whimsical patterns. They were kind of his calling card. He put the stars up wherever he went. Shyla lay on her back and stared at the stars, imagining Ryan beside her staring up at the same stars. She matched her breathing to her memories of his sleeping rhythms.

Morning dawned and Shyla had barely slept. Grace had to leave to go for work. Shyla told her it was okay. She would be okay. She had leftover food from the party to eat and the view of the whiteness in front of Ryan for her company. It was getting blurry around the edges. She thought that maybe today the battery pack might give out.

Trevor called her mid-morning. "We've spoken to the search and rescue team. The snow is still too heavy to get to him.

They are saying it might not be until after Christmas if the storm doesn't let up soon. We." He swallowed hard. "We have to discuss arrangements Shyla. Dad wants you to be part of it. When can you come over?"

"Later." She didn't know if she'd ever leave the apartment again. Without Ryan there to help her navigate the world it just all seemed so pointless.

She hung up from Trevor and called Ryan again. The snow was so thick on the screen that the phone's buzzing was almost inaudible, just the faintest noise. She had to crank the television volume way up to even hear that.

"Ryan? You promised. You said you'd be home for Christmas. You never broke a promise to me. Ever." She muffled her sob with the palm of her hand. "I love you. I miss you." She disconnected.

The exhaustion of her sleepless night and emotional trauma overtook her. Curled up on the couch, facing the television set and the view from her dead boyfriend's hat camera, Shyla slept.

She woke in that disoriented, half-aware state that is graciously visited upon the traumatized. The room was dark and at some point, she'd pulled the quilt over her and pushed the couch throw pillows into a makeshift nest. The television had gone dark. The camera batteries had probably died.

She called him again, intending to leave a loving message of farewell, to tell him all he'd meant to her and how much she loved him. She got three toneless beeps and then her phone cut out – the universal signal that the person she was calling was either out of range or out of battery power. Or in this case, both.

Her finger hovered over the power switch on the remote. By rights she should turn it off. She just couldn't.

She took a long bath and changed into a different

nightie. Tomorrow she would call Trevor and they could make arrangements for Ryan.

In the meantime, she knew she should eat. They had enough granola bars to sustain her for several years, but she didn't want that. She didn't want anything that reminded her of Ryan. She scrambled an egg and made a piece of toast and went to the living room. Maybe if she couldn't turn the television off, she could at least watch another channel, maybe lose herself in a mindless comedy.

The view from the camera had changed. It wasn't pitch black, as you'd expect from a dead battery. It was still dark, but it was lit intermittently by gobs of light streaking by. Shyla set her food on the end table and approached the television, studying the images.

Her phone rang shrilly, startling a shriek out of her.

"Hey." It was Trevor. "Is your TV still on Ryan?"

"Yeah."

"So, the fucking search and rescue couldn't get to him, but some fucker's raided his body and taken his shit?"

"What?"

"That's highway 40, Shyla, outside of Rickrack. Some fucker stole his hat and is walking the highway."

Shyla pulled her phone away and thumbed the tracking app open. It showed Ryan's cell phone was indeed somewhere along highway 40, heading east. Coming towards her.

She returned her phone to her ear.

"Shyla? You there?"

"Yes, Trevor. I'm here."

"You okay?" Loving concern tinged his usually gruff voice.

"Yes, Trevor."

"I think you should come over. It's Christmas Eve. You shouldn't be alone."

"I'll be okay, Trevor. I promise." She kept her eyes on the television, marking the procession of the cell phone along the darkened highway.

"Then at least come for Christmas dinner tomorrow, okay?"

Shyla hung up without making any promises about her attendance at Christmas. She knew how binding promises could be and she didn't want to make any she couldn't keep.

She dropped the thermostat until her apartment was freezing and she wrapped herself in blankets and sat on the couch, watching the television set fixedly.

The clock on her mantel dinged twelve times. It was Christmas Day.

The camera view showed a front door of an apartment building. Then a battered steel fire door. Then steps. One. Another. Another.

A wooden door with brass numbers screwed into it. Glow in the dark stars danced around the peephole.

Three firm knocks echoed through her apartment.

Promise kept.

LADY MARY

It wouldn't be a Christmas anthology without a ghost story...

"I know! Let's hold a séance!"

"On Christmas Night?" Brittany was shocked at her cousin Lilah's impudent suggestion.

"Sure! Why not!" Lilah bounced on the bed impatiently, her russet-coloured braids flying in the wake of her movement. "Come on. We gotta do something fun. This has got to be the most boring house ever."

Brittany had to admit Lilah was right. Gran's house had been more interesting when they were smaller. It was a yearly pilgrimage to spend the Christmas holidays with Gran. She had three sons and they always brought themselves and their families to sleep over Christmas Day until just before New Years' Eve. It was always a full house. Brittany always looked forward to these trips. She loved spending time with Lilah, who was a bit wild and always had ideas for things they could do.

Now that they were almost thirteen, there was very little here to amuse them. The novelty of their Christmas presents was already wearing off.

Gran and the rest of the family had gone to visit the neighbours but since Brittany, Lilah and Brittany's twin Destiny were deemed "old enough", they had been allowed to stay behind. It had been fun at first. They'd eaten cookies and made some videos to post on TikTok and done each other's hair and makeup and watched a super scary TV show on Lilah's tablet. Brittany hoped it hadn't scared Destiny too badly. Des wet the bed when she was scared.

But now, ninety minutes later, they were bored. Gran just had a basic television - no Netflix and no Disney+. She didn't even get YTV. There were just thirteen channels and there wasn't anything on any of them, unless you liked lame kid shows or boring black and white movies.

"Come on!" Lilah bounced again. "It's got to be better than sitting around here like three lumps."

"Have you ever done one?" Destiny asked.

Lilah's lips pursed in a derisive sneer. "Of course. Loads of times. We do it at sleepovers. One time we summoned the ghost of Gord Downie."

"Right." Brittany rolled her eyes. "As if the lead singer of the Tragically Hip has nothing better to do on a Saturday night than hang out with a bunch of twelve-year-olds."

"It was Friday night," Lilah snapped, "And we're all thirteen." She saw Brittany's blue eyes narrow in suspicion. "Almost thirteen," she hurried to clarify. Lilah's birthday was in January. The twins had their own birthdays coming up in March. Lilah was seven weeks older and loved to lord it over them.

"Still." Brittany shrugged dismissively. "You'd think he'd hang around somewhere better. Like models' bedrooms."

"Or BTS' dressing room," Destiny added. Her excessive fascination with the K-pop band was alternately amusing and exasperating to her twin and their cousin.

"I don't think he'd be as big a fan as someone else I know…" Brittany nudged her sister. It was part playful and part notice to stop mooning over the group. It got tiresome after awhile – like about five minutes.

"ANY-how…" Lilah emphasized the two syllables crisply. "We should have a séance before all the old people come home."

"Okay." Destiny was quick to agree. Both girls looked at Brittany, who finally shrugged.

"Why not." What was the worst that could happen?

"So how do we start?" Destiny looked at Lilah expectantly.

Lilah looked around the room the three girls were going to be sharing for the duration of their Christmas holidays. "Not here." Her nose wrinkled as she took in the piles of discarded clothing, half-eaten bags of chips and empty soda cans. "Somewhere with more... atmosphere..." She rubbed her chin thoughtfully. "I know – the coal cellar!"

"The coal cellar?" Brittany echoed. "It's so dark and creepy down there."

Lilah trilled a condescending laugh. "That's what makes it absolutely perfect," she stated. "It's dark and creepy and if they come home, we'll have time to clean up and pretend we were doing something else."

The coal cellar had been part of the house when it was built centuries ago. It wasn't used for anything now. Gran occasionally made noises around having someone come in to seal it off from the rest of the basement, but she hadn't gotten around to doing it yet.

"I don't think there's electricity down there." Brittany was stalling. It was dark and cold down there and there might be bugs.

"That's why we're going to get a candle." Lilah jumped up from the side of the bed and grabbed Brittany's hand. "Come on Britt, let's go!"

Brittany relented and allowed Lilah to drag her through the house. They paused in the dining room to scavenge one of the fat pillar candles from the array on the mantle and a book of matches from the sideboard.

The door to the coal cellar creaked open resentfully when Lilah pushed on it. Brittany was disappointed. She'd been hoping that the years of disuse had rusted it shut.

"The floor is dirty." Brittany looked down at the grimy floor, overlaid by a patina of dark grey coal dust from the past.

"I have a blanket." Destiny produced a blanket from their room. "I brought it with me," she added proudly, currying favour with their cool cousin Lilah.

"That was smart, Des." Lilah nodded her approval and set about creating the space for the séance. She laid the blanket down and set the lit candle in the middle. She sat down and reached her hands up expectantly to her cousins. "Well come on, then."

The three girls sat cross-legged on the blanket and reached to join their hands.

"Now who are we going to summon?" Lilah asked. Destiny opened her mouth eagerly and Lilah cautioned, "We can't use a séance to contact the living, Des. We won't be able to speak to BTS."

"Oh." Destiny sighed in disappointment. "Hey, how about Lady Mary?"

Lady Mary was a family legend. The very young first wife of a long-ago patriarch, it was rumoured that she'd been strangled by her husband on Christmas Day after he accused her of having an affair. She hadn't been having an affair at all. Rumour was he'd murdered her to inherit her sizeable dowry without being saddled by a wife who was still in her teens. The family stories claimed she still roamed the halls, looking for another body to take over so she could exact her revenge on her murderer and his descendants.

"Lady Mary is perfect," Lilah proclaimed. "And on Christmas Day too. What do you think, Britt?"

Brittany shrugged. If they were going to sit on the dirty floor in a candlelit room and pretend that they were summoning a ghost, the spirit of a girl who had died in this house on this night centuries ago seemed to be as good a choice as any.

"Close your eyes," Lilah urged the other two. "It's easier to concentrate."

Brittany reluctantly closed her eyes. She was starting to regret going along with Lilah.

"Oh spirits," Lilah intoned deeply. "Spirits are you with us?"

Brittany strained to hear something, but the house was silent.

"Spirits." Lilah tried again. "Is there one who wants to speak with us? We are trying to reach Lady Mary."

Still nothing. "I don't think it—" Brittany started to speak and then a loud "bang" echoed through the room.

"I think one is coming through." They had all opened their eyes at the sound. "Close your eyes, let's try to get them here." Lilah closed her eyes again. "Spirits! We hear you and welcome you on this night. This very special night. This Christmas Day..." She drew out the last word, making it echo hollowly around the dim room.

There were a series of scuffles and thuds that seemed to come from all around them. Brittany yelped and tried to pull her hands free. Lilah tightened her grasp.

"Don't break the circle," she warned, "It's very dangerous. You could get possessed by a ghost."

Brittany stopped trying to yank away and instead tightened her grip to the point that Destiny whimpered, "Ow! Britt, loosen up a bit!"

A draft eddied through the room. Brittany opened her eyes again. The candle flame was flickering wildly. She looked around the room, wondering if the door had blown open. It was still firmly shut behind them.

Movement in far corner of the room caught her attention. A figure shuffled out of the darkness.

"Guys..." Brittany tugged on the hands holding hers. "Guys!

Someone's here!"

Destiny gasped and Lilah giggled.

"It actually worked…" Lilah cleared her throat, and her voice took on a more sombre tone. "Lady Mary are you with us?"

"Yessss…" the voice was deep and gravelly.

"What are you wearing?" Destiny blurted, "It looks like a sheet from one of the rooms upstairs."

"Shroud…" The harsh whisper drifted around the room. Brittany felt chills run along her spine. She gasped as she felt the cold surrounding her. It felt like ice cold arms were hugging her from behind. A cold breath frosted over her cheek from a low voice whispering in her ear.

Brittany wiggled a bit in her spot, shaking off the coldness that had surrounded her so completely. As soon as it came upon her, it was gone, leaving behind small frissons of chilliness playing over her shoulders and her back. It felt as though her skin was crawling with little icy trickles.

Destiny looked at her sister. "What's up with you?"

"It's freezing in here," Brittany complained. "Can't you feel it?"

"I'm fine," Destiny said. She dismissed her twin and turned back to the apparition looming over their circle. "Are you really Lady Mary?" she asked the ghost.

"Yessss…."

"Why are you here?" Lilah took over the questioning. She'd summoned the ghost. It was her right to do all the asking. Or so she thought.

The figure shuffled closer, standing just outside the wavering circle of light cast by the candle. "Summoned…"

"Why is she only saying one word?" Destiny blurted.

Lilah shushed her harshly. "She's a ghost, dummy. It's hard for them to be in this world. One-word answers are likely all she can manage."

The ghost hissed, "Yessss…."

Lilah lifted her chin triumphantly. "See? Boy are you dumb sometimes, Des."

Brittany shook off the pervasive chill and tried to remember some of the accounts about sightings of Lady Mary's ghost. They were always preceded with a strong scent of lavender. "There wasn't any scent of lavender," she pointed out to Lilah.

"Probably because we summoned her." Lilah put on an air of authority. "She isn't here of her own free will."

The ghost agreed again with another sibilant, "Yesssss…"

"So that's why she's also missing the red shawl?" The ghost of Lady Mary was also rumoured to feature her red shawl – the murder weapon – wound around her neck and shoulders.

"Brittany, stop," Lilah snapped. "It's the ghost."

"Ask her why she roams the halls," Destiny suggested.

"Restless…." the ghost whispered.

"Why can't you rest?" Lilah asked.

"Revenge…" the ghost moaned. It shuffled a bit closer. The glow of the candle highlighted the embroidered hyacinths at the border of the shroud. Very fancy. And familiar. Brittany tried to remember where she'd seen it before. But before she could figure it out, Lilah asked another question.

"Why are you here?"

"Wa-a-a-ant…" The ghost's voice raised to a wail like nails on the blackboard.

"What do you want?" Lilah demanded.

The ghost moved quickly. Her voice rose to an ear-splitting

shriek, and she grabbed for Destiny. "YOU!"

The three girls screeched and tumbled over each other in their rush to get out of the coal cellar. The door slammed shut in their wake and they bolted up the stairs, not even noticing the other figure lurking in the corner of the furnace room opposite the stairs.

Divested of the shroud and looking more like Lilah's older sister Meagan, the apparition wandered out of the coal cellar. Fabric was bundled up under her arm and she held the candle in her hand. "They ran up so quick, it blew the candle out," she giggled.

A dark figure emerged from the furnace room. "Are you feeling better now? How's your headache?"

Meagan grinned at her cousin Freddie. The two of them had been thick as thieves since they were toddlers.

"Yes, my headache is gone now. Thanks for driving me back from the Johnstons'." She giggled. "I guess the cure for a migraine is scaring the pants off of my sister and our cousins."

"How did you know they'd be down here having a séance?" Freddie cocked his head, listening to the panicked cries from upstairs. They faded as the three girls ran up to the second floor and then the slamming of the distant bedroom door cut them off altogether.

"Lilah's been obsessed with them lately," Meagan shrugged, "It's all she talks about. I knew as soon as everyone was gone, they'd be doing one."

"But how did you know they'd be down here?" Freddie nodded to the empty coal cellar.

"It's the spookiest spot in the house by far. Good atmosphere. And I knew how to sneak in through the outside door. I used it when I was here over the summer, and I was sneaking out after bedtime to meet boys."

"Right. Let's get upstairs, get that sheet back on the bed in my bedroom and then pretend we're just coming home from the party." A brief glow illuminated his face as headlights from the adults' returning cars splashed across the basement windows. "I think we're just in time. We can mix in with the others. The kids will never know it was us."

Megan giggled again. "I'll be surprised if we see any of them tonight. They're probably all upstairs hiding in their beds."

For the most part, she wasn't wrong. Mindful of Des' nightly proclivities when she was scared, they'd pressed her to sleep on the rollaway cot that was unfolded at the foot of the room's double bed. She was huddled into a tight ball, pillow over her head and humming BTS songs under her breath. On one side of the double bed, Lilah hid under the covers, blankets pulled up around her ears and pillow wedged tightly over her head.

On the other side of the bed, Brittany lay on her back, staring solidly up at the ceiling. She lay there rigid and unmoving for the next couple of hours. Around her the rest of the family bid each other good night, performed their nightly trips to the bathroom and last raids on the fridge, and then finally settled into sleep. The eventual silence of the house was broken only by the occasional soft snore, creak of bedsprings as someone turned over and the soft whispers from Gran's room because she liked to sleep with her television on.

Brittany finally sat up and swung her legs over the side of the bed. The scent of lavender hung heavily around her. She reached for the red scarf draped over the mirror of the dresser.

It was time to go to work.

LIMBS

Nobody ever thinks of how the tree feels.

At night when the lights are off and the room is dark except for the faint glow of the night light, I can still see the distant hills where I came from. I can remember the feeling of the wind sweeping through my glory, bringing tidings of the weather and scents of the meadow. I was naked then, and unknown. One of the many standing sentinel in silence as the thick snow coated us in icy layers year after year, then kissed by the spring breezes and baked by the summer sun blazing away above. In the fall, our fellow dwellers shook off their rustling adornments to stand naked, reaching proudly out into the chilly air while we stayed cloaked and cozy year-round in dark green and brown.

I'm adorned now and adored. At least I think so. The ones who live in this stone and wood place seem to spend a lot of time admiring me. I keep hearing them say words like, "lovely" and "radiant". Even though my limbs sometimes tremble from the effort of holding the gaudy baubles aloft and my base aches from the unkindness they visited upon me, there's this new sensation I feel when they gaze at me. Inside I feel warm and welcome, like a birdling in a nest.

We all have a bad side, the side where the wind tears a bit more deeply, the side where the creatures of the fields scavenge for pieces for their nests or tidbits to eat. It's the side we are ashamed of, where our foliage is thinner, our branches less symmetrical. The ones who stole me from my home recognize this and position me so that my ugliness is concealed, and they concentrate the prettiest adornments on my most verdant sides.

I've seen others taken from our rows, usually a couple of them every winter and now I wonder if this was their ultimate destination. If so, shouldn't they have been here to greet me? The receptacle where my tortured end rests bears scrapes and stains that might indicate the passage of the others – but where have they gone?

There is coldness in this place where I stand. It laps around my nether end, almost like the streams that swell and run by us when the snow melts every spring. It provides me some sustenance, even though it tastes of the flat chemical smell of the walls that surround it. It isn't as nourishing as the rains that fall from the sky, but it is enough to slow down the inevitable.

There is one exciting night where the family gathers around me. The larger ones read a story to the smaller ones. A captive audience, I listen. It's a story about a man with reindeer and something called a "sleigh". The cadence of the words is soothing and my limbs sway and rustle in response.

After the story, the wee ones open brightly coloured boxes to reveal new sleeping foliage. They squeal in delight and run to put them on.

When they come back, they make a big show of putting out a plate with some round discs on it and a receptacle half-full of white creamy liquid. Then the littles leave again.

After a while, the biggers pull brightly coloured boxes out of the closet and pile them around me. I try to stand up straighter, proud to be receiving even more decorations. One of the biggers takes several bites of a disc and the other drinks half the liquid. He makes a face and says, "Yuck, lukewarm milk." They laugh as they leave the room and let me have my thoughts.

It doesn't seem to be very much time before the family comes tumbling back into the room again. The littles tear the coloured packages open, and shrieks and squeals rend the air.

The whole day is a confusing blur. After the littles have

calmed down, the family welcomes other people and there are more boxes, more tearing, more shrieking. A lot of the new people compliment me – how full I am, how green and how lovely. I preen and stand up straighter.

The next few days after that one are quieter. The littles spend a lot of time playing outside. My water replenishments start coming slower with longer spaces in between. The inevitable begins to happen. I can feel the dryness rustling, the slow rot spreading through the green.

One night the biggers put the littles to bed and sit staring at me. Finally, one of them sighs. "I think we'd better get it done."

To my shock, they spend the evening taking all my lovely ornaments off. I try hard to hold onto my favourite – a bejeweled cardinal that reminds me of the gracefully boisterous birds that flitted around us, twitting their songs proudly. He tugs harder, dislodging a brace of my needles to retrieve my prize and put it carefully in a box. There is another one left behind, a misshapen gaudy lump that is vaguely human-shaped. He reaches for it, then withdraws his hand.

"I'm leaving this one. It's stuck to the branch and if we don't have that ugly Santa your sister brought back from Mexico, is anyone going to notice?" She agrees with him and goes back to carefully placing my pretties in a box.

When they are done, I am slumping in the corner, practically naked and ashamed. The fact that they left me with one ornament, the ugliest of them all, in some ways is more insulting than if they'd stolen them all away. I bristle with rage, but they ignore me. Did the rest of mine come to this ignominious end? Were they this devastated and deplored? Is that why none of them were here to greet me when these people stole me from my tidy row and subjected me to the glitz and the glory and then the anger and the agony of this existence?

"I'll put it out tomorrow for the garbage truck." The light

goes out, leaving me in total darkness. Not even a bit of a shine reflecting from my ornaments.

They left the cord that provided the glow of my lights out. I can see there is a spot that is frayed away – where I can almost see the spark and thrum of the energy contained within. I have a dry needle just hovering over the bare spot. It can be released with a thought.

If I'm going, they're coming with me.

ACKNOWLEDGEMENTS

It's time for the "necessary evils" as poor Ry would say.

First of all, thank you to my beloved David – my rock, my everything. He's my biggest cheerleader and also a major pain the ass when I need to be motivated to keep going. I love you so much. Thank you isn't enough.

Thank you to Krystyne, my alpha reader. She reads everything that I write and provides tons of feedback. She's also the genius responsible for setting up my blog (www.lenorewrites.ca). If you happen by there, you'll get my insights on writing, some other snippets of stories, as well as a ringside seat to the insanity and chaos that is my life. If you're in need of anything social media or digital, she's awesome at it. www.getseenonline.ca

My children Joseph and Audrey are the lights of my life. Thanks for being understanding when Mama shuts herself away to write… or when she's in the room but you know by the look in her eyes she's really miles away watching a man being menaced by nutcrackers.

The community on www.deadlinesforwriters.com deserves a shoutout. Many of these stories began there as part of the monthly challenges. The feedback I received shaped the first edits.

Speaking of online communities, the group at Writers' Flow Studio run by the amazing Rhonda Douglas have been tireless in their enthusiasm and support. It is truly a remarkable environment. Thank you to this group of fierce, talented and funny ladies.

Tobin Elliott, who is a powerhouse horror writer in his own right, needs recognition here for his relentless badgering every time I saw him. And for being my own personal writing boogeyman that my husband could threaten me with. "Do you need me to tell Tobin on you?" was a frequent refrain every time it seemed I was stalling out in my progress towards publication.

My final thank you is to you. Thank you for taking a chance on this book. Thank you for reading it. If you enjoyed it (or if you didn't and you want to have a say about it), please leave me a review.

Until next time…Merry Christmas.

Manufactured by Amazon.ca
Acheson, AB